**'It's delicious,' Katie said, sipping the hot liquid and savouring the aroma. 'I could almost be tempted to work here just for the coffee alone.'**

Alex laughed. 'So I'm making some headway at last. Wonderful. Do you want a refill?'

'Let's not get too excited.' She lifted her gaze. 'I don't often give in that easily to temptation.'

'You don't?' He started towards her as she put the cup down onto the worktop, and came to a halt just beside her. His gaze shimmered over her, pausing to linger momentarily on her soft, feminine curves. His smoky grey glance spoke volumes, his eyes glimmering with darting lights that tantalised and teased all at the same time. 'That's a real shame. I would so like to have been able to tempt you.'

Katie was suddenly flustered by his nearness. His body was so close to hers that they were almost touching…almost, but not quite. 'I didn't… I meant…'

# TOP-NOTCH DOCS

*He's not just the boss, he's the best there is!*

These heroes aren't just doctors,
they're life-savers.

These heroes aren't just surgeons,
they're skilled masters. Their talent and
reputation are admired by all.

These heroes are devoted to their patients.
They'll hold the littlest babies in their arms,
and melt the hearts of all who see.

These heroes aren't just
medical professionals. They're the
men of your dreams.

*He's not just the boss, he's the best there is*

# A CONSULTANT BEYOND COMPARE

BY

JOANNA NEIL

All the characters in this book have no existence outside the imagination of the author, and have no relation whatsoever to anyone bearing the same name or names. They are not even distantly inspired by any individual known or unknown to the author, and all the incidents are pure invention.



First published in Great Britain 2008
Harlequin Mills & Boon Limited,
Eton House, 18-24 Paradise Road, Richmond, Surrey TW9 1SR



ISBN: 978 0 263 19871 3

Set in Times Roman 10½ on 12¾ pt
15-0208-47210

Printed and bound in Great Britain
by Antony Rowe Ltd, Chippenham, Wiltshire

When **Joanna Neil** discovered Mills & Boon®, her life-long addiction to reading crystallised into an exciting new career writing Medical™ Romance. Her characters are probably the outcome of her varied lifestyle, which includes working as a clerk, typist, nurse and infant teacher. She enjoys dressmaking and cooking at her Leicestershire home. Her family includes a husband, son and daughter, an exuberant yellow Labrador and two slightly crazed cockatiels. She currently works with a team of tutors at her local education centre to provide creative writing workshops for people interested in exploring their own writing ambitions.

**Recent titles by the same author:**

THE DOCTOR'S LONGED-FOR FAMILY
THE CONSULTANT'S SURPRISE CHILD
EMERGENCY AT RIVERSIDE HOSPITAL
THE LONDON CONSULTANT'S RESCUE
HER VERY SPECIAL CONSULTANT

## CHAPTER ONE

THE ring tone from Katie's mobile phone sounded, growing louder and more insistent with each passing second. She frowned, flipping open the phone and peering down at the screen in front of her.

What now? Was it totally impossible for her to have five minutes of peace and quiet to enable her to think things through, without someone desperately seeking her attention or needing her to do something for them right away?

Then again, the whole day had been a disaster from start to finish, hadn't it, so why should anything change now? From the moment she had arrived for work at the rehab centre that morning, things had been going steadily downhill.

First there had been the discovery that one of the workmen on site had drilled through a water pipe, and as if that wasn't enough to put the seal on the day, shortly afterwards one of the builders doing the renovations had taken a nasty tumble from the main roof.

It was bad enough that the poor man had broken his fall on a lower sloping timber roof and then crashed through it into the patients' sun lounge, but it could have been far worse. It was only just short of a miracle that no one had been sitting in there at the time.

'Well, at least we've managed to find alternative places for all of our stroke patients,' Mandy, Katie's boss, said, coming out into the garden in search of her.

Katie had found herself a calm nook by the arbour, where she could sit on a bench and take in the fresh, clean air. The warmth of the summer sun filtered through the branches of the trees, caressing her arms, making her feel a little less stressed.

'They don't seem to have been too badly affected by all the upheaval and I've made sure that they'll be able to go on with their rehabilitation in their new situations.' Mandy heaved a sigh. 'None of this bodes well for us, though. With the patients' sun lounge in a shambles and a hole drilled through the water pipe, it looks as though we'll have to close down until the renovations are complete. Of course, they're going to take much longer now.'

'Yes, I thought that might be the result.' Feeling a little more in control of herself now, Katie straightened up and brushed back the long sweep of her chestnut hair with her fingers. 'Has there been any news on the builder?'

'Apparently he's in Theatre now, having his leg reset. The doctor confirmed your diagnosis—he had suffered a heart attack, but they think it was a mild one and with proper care he should be all right, given time.'

Mandy gave Katie a long look. 'I was amazed at how you leapt into action. I'm sure you saved his life. I can't think what you're doing working in rehab when you have those skills at your fingertips. You should be in a hospital emergency department, where your talents would be recognised.'

The thought of that sent a minor chill along Katie's spine. She had made up her mind that she would never again work in A and E, and it had been some months since she had properly used her medical skills. From the moment she had come across the injured man, though, her actions had been triggered as if by remote control. She hadn't given it a second thought. It was as though she had been an automaton, going through a series of well-rehearsed actions without giving them any conscious attention.

In a way, the man was fortunate, because after he'd fallen through the broken timbers, he had somehow managed to land on a wicker sofa. Any other kind of landing might have resulted in him not being around any longer to tell the tale.

Katie had rushed over to him, picking her way through the debris of wood and broken glass, and had immediately started to attend to his injuries, while Mandy had phoned for the ambulance. All Katie's A and E skills had come back to her in that moment as she'd applied pressure to his wounds to stem the bleeding. It had only been afterwards that she had broken out into a cold sweat.

Mandy frowned as the phone continued to ring. 'Aren't you going to get that?'

'Yes, I suppose I must.' Katie pressed a button and the noise stopped instantly. For a moment or two she sat and simply absorbed the silence, a sense of relief washing over her.

'I'm glad he's not in too bad a way.' It had been fairly obvious to her from the outset that the builder must have had some kind of heart attack, and she had concentrated all her efforts on doing what she could to stabilise his condition until the ambulance had arrived. It had only been after she had seen him safely handed over to the care of the paramedics that she had been able to take full stock of what had happened, and shortly after that shock had begun to set in.

Her whole body had been racked by tremors and she had made her way outside to this bench where she felt that at least for a while she would be safe from prying eyes.

Mandy nodded. 'Me, too. I just wanted to let you know that all the arrangements are in place. We're officially closed down for the foreseeable future.'

'I'm sorry. I know how much effort you've put into the centre.'

Mandy nodded. 'I'll go and make a pot of tea.' A faint smile crossed her mouth. 'When in doubt, go and put the kettle on. At least there was some water left in it when the supply was cut off. I'll leave you to take your call in peace,' she added when Katie's mobile started ringing yet again.

'Thanks.' Katie lifted the phone to her ear as she watched her go.

A man was saying urgently, 'Hello? Hello…?' A note of impatience threaded his words. 'Are you there? Is that Miss Sorenson…Katie Sorenson?'

Katie frowned at the unfamiliar male voice. She didn't recognise the number that showed up on her display screen, and if this was someone who was about to try to sell her something, he would very soon find himself listening to a disconnection tone.

'Yes, I'm Katie Sorenson.'

'Ah, at last…that's good.' The man paused, giving her time to contemplate the deep, beautifully modulated quality of his voice. He sounded as though he was youngish, in his thirties maybe, but she still didn't have any idea who he might be.

'Is it?' she murmured, at a loss. 'Perhaps you could enlighten me? Do I know you?'

'No, I don't believe so, but I think perhaps we should meet. I'm at a café near the railway station in Windermere and I have your sister here with me—she tells me her name is Jessica, and that she's thirteen years old. Is that right?'

'My sister?' Katie's blue eyes widened in shock. 'You can't be serious? What is she doing in Windermere?' She checked his phone number on her mobile's screen once more, and a shiver ran through her as she tried to work out what exactly was happening. Something was definitely wrong. What was Jessica doing some ten miles away, sitting in a café with a strange man?

Then she pulled herself together. Surely she was letting her imagination run away with her? Anyone who was trying to abduct Jessica would hardly take the trouble to phone her, would he? Even so, she said with a hint of suspicion in her tone, 'How is it that you're with my sister?'

She caught the wry inflection in his voice as he answered that. 'I've just come across her, trying to hitch a lift at the roadside, and I have a strong feeling that she isn't going to be safe, left to her own devices. She said that she was trying to get home to you, but she was lost. If that's the case, and you are who you say you are, I would very much prefer to hand her over to you in person.'

Katie pulled in a deep breath. 'I don't believe this is happening. Is this a joke?'

'Far from it, I'm afraid.' There was a note of censure in his voice as he added, 'I can't imagine why you would allow a 13-year-old to wander about on her own so far from home, but she assures me that you are the one who is supposed to be looking after her.' He was silent for a moment, as though he was leaving time for his comments to sink in.

Katie frowned. Why would Jessica have told him that? Her sister lived with their parents, a hundred or so miles away from the Lake District, in a town near the mouth of the Humber. What on earth was going on?

The man was speaking once more, his tone a little brisk now. 'I'd come over to you, but I really don't think that would be appropriate. I'm a stranger to your sister and I don't want my actions to be misconstrued, so I'd appreciate it if you would come and fetch her.'

Katie's mouth firmed. 'Let me speak to her, please.' She still had to be convinced that this wasn't some kind of elaborate prank.

There was a momentary pause, and then Jessica's voice sounded in her ear. 'Katie, please, don't be cross with me. I didn't mean to cause any trouble. I got a bit lost, that's all.'

Katie pulled in a sharp breath. 'More than a bit, I'd say. What are you doing this far from home, and what are you doing with a strange man?'

Jessica made a faint gulping sound. 'He asked me for your number and said he would get in touch with you. I didn't have any credit left on my phone, you see, and then the battery went flat and I'd used up all my money, and anyway I'd already tried to reach you on your home phone and you weren't there.'

'No, that's because I'm at work. That still doesn't tell me what you're doing out at Windermere.'

'No, I…I know it doesn't…but I promise I'll explain everything when I see you.' Jessica's voice trailed off awkwardly, and Katie guessed she hadn't told this man the full truth of the situation. 'Will you come and fetch me?'

'Yes, of course I will. Let me speak to this man.'

Jessica handed the phone back to her rescuer, and Katie forced herself to take a slow, calming breath. 'Perhaps you could tell me exactly where you are and I'll come over to you,' she said briskly.

He gave her directions, and added on a cool note, 'I hope you'll drop everything and come straight away. I was on my way to a meeting and I'd still like to be able to get there some time before it ends if it's at all possible.'

He didn't sound as though he had very much faith in her, and Katie stifled a sharp response. 'I'm sorry about your meeting,' she told him in a strained tone. 'I have a twenty-minute or so drive ahead of me, but I'll be there as soon as possible.'

Clearly the man had a busy schedule. So had she, up until now, but from what Mandy had been saying that had all come to an abrupt end. There was little doubt that she was going to be out of work from today.

In the staff kitchen, Mandy had already poured the tea, but Katie hurriedly swallowed it down and went to find her bag. 'I have to go,' she said. 'An emergency just cropped up and I need to go and pick up my young sister.'

'Your sister?' Mandy raised a brow. 'I didn't know you had any family around here.'

Katie's expression was rueful. 'Neither did I.' She glanced across the table at her friend. 'Will you be all right here?'

Mandy nodded. 'We've done about as much as we can with the clearing-up operations, so I'll probably just send the rest of the staff home.' She made a wry face. 'I don't think there'll be much point in any of us coming in for the next few months. I'm sorry.'

'I know.' Katie touched her shoulder in a gesture of sympathy. 'I'll give you a call later on,' she murmured.

Mandy nodded, and Katie hurried out to her car.

Her mind was racing as she drove towards

Windermere. What on earth was Jessica doing out here? The shock of this news, coming on top of everything else that had happened today had left her feeling thoroughly churned up inside. She had hoped to put all this kind of stress behind her, but now she was going through the same kind of anxiety she had experienced back in Humberside in those last months when her contract at the hospital had come to an end. Her emotions were all over the place.

Caught up in traffic a few minutes later, Katie had time to reflect on all that had gone wrong at her former hospital post. Everyone had expected that her position as Senior House Officer in A and E would be made permanent, but after what had happened in the operating theatre there were some who believed she had made a mistake, putting her patient's life at risk, and from then onwards her career progress had been in question.

It hadn't helped that her consultant had been unapproachable and stiff-lipped. 'The patient might have bled to death,' he said.

'But he didn't. At least I managed to stem the bleeding.' She frowned as the nightmare situation came back to haunt her. 'The man was in a bad way when I first saw him, and I tried to get in touch with you before he went to Theatre. I needed back-up, but your answering service said you weren't available.' As a junior doctor, she ought to have been able to call on her consultant for guidance.

He had turned on her. 'I hope you're not going to use that as an excuse,' he'd said tersely. 'I should be able to rely on the competence of the members of my team. If you're not up to the job, I think you should start to look for another post.'

It was a devastating blow to her hopes and dreams but, worse than that, what had happened in Theatre had thoroughly shaken her up. The patient had been critically ill to begin with, and the massive bleed into his lungs could have killed him.

The nurse who had been assisting took her to one side. 'These things happen,' Helen told her. 'It wasn't your fault. It's well known that there are sometimes complications with the type of catheter you were using, and when the worst happened you did everything you could to pull the man through. You saved him.'

'But his recovery is going to take much longer than it should,' Katie whispered, still shaken in the aftermath of events.

Her boss hadn't been in Theatre with her when the patient's pulmonary artery had been punctured, and when the patient's family had asked about the man's condition he had brushed their concerns to one side, telling them that he had suffered an unexpected bleed. Of course, questions had followed after that.

'You should pray that they don't sue,' he had told her.

Whatever the eventual outcome, it was clear to Katie that he wouldn't be supportive of her. He would watch his own back and by making sure that her contract wasn't renewed he could rest easy.

And now she was out of work once again. It was distressing, to say the least, because she had come to the

Lake District in the hope of putting all that upset behind her once and for all.

It had taken her a while to get over the upheaval of having to change her job, she had tried her hand at various kinds of work back home before settling on this post further afield.

The change of scene would do her good, she had hoped, and it would give her the boost she needed to help her to get back into the swing of things. Now that dream, too, had come to an end, and she was left with yet another problem to contend with.

The miles swept by as she drove towards Windermere, and soon she could see the vast stretch of the lake spread out before her. There were boats dotted about on the water that sparkled in the sunlight, and all around were hills and valleys swathed in green, with pretty villages of stone and slate houses nestled against the backdrop of trees.

It was a beautiful, tranquil setting, and she ought to be glad that she was here and able to appreciate its peacefulness, but as she headed towards the railway station and parked her car, she was hardly aware of that.

She walked over to the café the man had mentioned. Tables and chairs had been set up outside on a terraced area in front of the building so that customers could enjoy the summer sunshine. A few people were relaxing there, sipping coffee or cold drinks, and as she scanned their faces, she discovered that her sister was amongst them.

Jessica was sitting tensely upright next to a man

who was wearing a crisp blue shirt and immaculate dark-coloured trousers. His discarded jacket was placed casually over the back of his seat.

Although he was partially turned away from her, Katie could see that his hair was black and close cut in an attractive fashion, so that it framed his features and outlined the angular lines of his face.

Just then Jessica looked up and saw Katie approaching the café. She stood up and started towards her, moving awkwardly as though she wasn't quite sure what her reception would be.

'Katie…Katie, oh, I'm so glad you came.' She hesitated. 'I'm so sorry. I didn't mean to fetch you out of work, but everything went wrong and I was lost and I didn't know what to do.'

'It's all right.' Katie put her arms around her sister and ran a soothing hand over the girl's silky brown curls. 'I've found you now. We'll sort everything out.'

Jessica's body slumped with relief as some of the tension left her. She clung to Katie for a few moments longer, and then eased back, her expression taking on a strained appearance.

She said softly, 'I knew your address, and I was trying to come over to your house, but this man stopped me and made me wait with him here. I'd have been all right, honest, but he wouldn't let me carry on.' She lowered her voice and whispered confidentially, 'He thinks you and I had an argument and that I was running away. I daren't tell him what really happened. I thought he might put me on a train and send me back home.'

Katie nodded. 'Yes, I can see why you kept quiet, but he was right to stop you, you know. You might have ended up in a terrible state. You're lucky that he turned out to be one of the good guys.' She frowned. 'We must go and let him know that you're safe now.'

Jessica chewed at her lower lip. Reluctantly, she allowed Katie to lead her back to the table where she had been sitting, and for the first time Katie managed to take a proper look at her sister's saviour.

He stood up, unfurling his long body with a supple grace that added to the immediate impression of lithe vitality. He took her breath away. He was tall and fit-looking, flat-stomached, with broad shoulders and a lean physique that she guessed was honed to perfection.

He was staring at her in return, a look of startled surprise coming into his grey-blue eyes. 'Do I know you?' he asked. 'You look somehow familiar.' And once again that deeply satisfying voice shimmered over her consciousness. It made her feel warm all over, and quickened her pulse so that she had to quell a sudden surge of nervous tension.

'No, I don't think so,' she murmured. But then again, there was something about him that struck a chord with her too, and she looked at him again, more closely this time. Did she know him from somewhere?

She dismissed the thought. 'I must thank you for taking care of my sister,' she said softly. 'I'm really very grateful to you. I can't imagine what she was thinking.'

'It appeared to me that she was desperate to get away,' he said, his gaze drifting over her. 'I can't begin to understand what must have gone on in order for her to feel that way, and yet from the way you greeted one another it seems that she's either changed her mind or learned a lesson. I hope you'll be able to resolve things between you.'

'Yes, well, let's hope so. She's very young, and life can be confusing for teenagers at the best of times, can't it? I don't know about you, but my childhood was no bed of roses, and I expect we've all gone through difficult phases at some time or other in our lives.'

He nodded, and gave her a thoughtful look. 'I suppose that's true enough.' He studied her features for a moment or two, and then added, 'Do you think you'll have any difficulty sorting out whatever it was that went wrong between you? Perhaps I could act as an intermediary and help you to find a way to work things out?'

Katie wavered for a moment or two. 'That really won't be necessary. I'm sure we'll manage to find a solution to whatever has gone wrong.' It wasn't a lie, and why should she burden this stranger with the intricacies of her home life? He had stepped in and helped out, and she was grateful to him for that, but it didn't mean that he was entitled to hear her life story. 'Anyway, didn't you say that you had a meeting to go to?'

He glanced at his watch. 'I doubt there would be any point in attempting to get there now.' His gaze settled on her. 'Perhaps you were delayed in setting out?'

A guilty flush ran over her cheeks. 'I hit some traffic on the way. I'm not quite sure what happened, but there was a tailback and I had to find another route, otherwise I would have been here quicker.'

He nodded. 'I dare say it couldn't be helped.' He glanced at Jessica. 'How do you feel about going home with your sister? Are you going to be all right or do you want me to stay around for a while to help you out?'

Jessica had the grace to look shamefaced. 'I'll be fine,' she mumbled. 'I'm sorry to have caused you so much trouble.'

He was reaching for his jacket as she spoke, and now he started to shrug into it. 'It's no problem,' he said. Then he added on an afterthought, 'If you feel that you need to talk to anyone any time, you could always ring me. I'll give you my number.' Taking a notecase from his inside jacket pocket, he handed Jessica a card. 'Keep it safe. You can ring me any time. If I'm not on hand right away, I'll always get back to you.'

Jessica glanced at the card and then slipped it into her pocket. 'Thank you.'

Katie wasn't sure whether to feel grateful to him for his concern or affronted by it. This man had taken the trouble to keep her young sister out of danger, but at the same time he seemed to be implying that Katie might be the source of all the trouble in the first place. She sent him a spiky glance, her blue eyes glittering.

'She'll be fine with me,' she murmured, keeping an even tone.

'Good. I'm glad to hear it.' He sent her an appraising look. 'I can't help thinking, though, that something must have gone very wrong for her to have felt the need to run away in the first place, and she was certainly very reticent in talking about it. Perhaps you'll be able to talk things through and make a better go of things.'

'We will,' Katie answered him stiffly. 'Thank you again for everything you've done. I do appreciate the way you've looked after her for me.'

He nodded briefly. 'I have her number and your address, so I'll keep in touch,' he said in a low voice. 'I'd like to satisfy myself that she's doing all right.'

Katie's chin lifted a notch. Was that a warning to her that he was prepared to keep an eye on things? Just how far did he mean to take his good Samaritan responsibilities?

She gave him a humourless smile. 'Thanks again,' she said. 'We won't impose on your time any longer. I should be starting on my way home before the traffic gets any worse. I'm just hoping that whatever caused the hold-up has been cleared by now.'

'Me, too. Now that attending my meeting is out of the question, I'll be heading back in your direction. If what Jessica tells me is correct, it looks as though we both live in the same area, around Ambleside.'

Katie groaned inwardly and tried not to let her emotions show in her face. She might have known that would be the case. With the way her luck was going today, perhaps it was only to be expected. Clearly she was not going to be free of this man for some time to come. Perhaps all she could do would be to forget that he had ever been around. The last thing she needed was more condemnation from men who thought they had the upper hand. She turned away from him.

'Goodbye, Jessica,' he said.

Jessica nodded to him and made a muted response before turning to follow Katie to her car.

'Let's go,' Katie said, sliding in behind the wheel of her ancient car and waiting while Jessica strapped herself in. She was anxious to put this whole incident behind her, but as she pulled away from the kerb she was all too aware of the man following behind in a sleek, midnight-blue convertible.

## CHAPTER TWO

KATIE turned the car on to the north road, heading towards Ambleside. She barely noticed the bracken-covered hills and heather-clad knolls, or the wide, U-shaped valleys that had been carved out by ice all those aeons ago. Her thoughts were taken up with the events of the day.

She still carried with her the brooding, dark image of Jessica's rescuer, and it was troubling that he seemed to have misgivings about her ability to care for her sister. She had always thought of herself as a capable, independent individual, but lately her confidence had taken a battering. How could any of this be happening to her?

'You will let me stay with you, won't you, Katie?' Her younger sister turned earnest, pleading eyes on her and Katie felt her heart give a painful twist. 'I promise I won't be any trouble, but I can't go back home, I can't. You won't send me back there, will you?'

'But you're only thirteen, Jess,' Katie answered, in

what she hoped was a soothing voice, 'and you're a long way from home. Mum and Dad will be worried about you.'

'No, they won't. They don't care about me as long as I'm out of their hair. They'll just go on arguing, and shouting at one another like they always do. It's horrible. I won't go back.'

'Of course they care about you.' Katie frowned as she glanced at the road ahead. Perhaps she shouldn't have taken this route. She had hoped to avoid problems, but traffic was building up, and it was beginning to occur to her that whatever had delayed her earlier on the journey to Windermere had merely been the overspill from what was happening up ahead. There must have been an accident of some sort, because in the distance she could see the flashing lights from ambulances that were parked by the roadside. A couple of police vehicles were stationed nearby.

Jessica made a face. 'No, they don't. They're not going to miss me at all. They hardly ever notice I'm around, unless it's because they think I'm getting in their way. Dad's never had any time for me. He's always at work or off out somewhere and as for Mum…well, she's too busy worrying about her own problems, so she'll be glad there's one less person to bother about.' She sighed. 'You know how they are. They're always arguing about something or other. Isn't that why you left home and went off to medical school? You were glad to get away, weren't you?'

Katie's mouth made a wry shape. 'It was a bit different for me. After all, Mum divorced my father when I was just a bit younger than you are now, and when she married again—well, it felt a bit odd. Things were never quite the same.' She smiled at Jessica. 'But then you came along, and it was lovely for me to have a baby sister.'

Jessica's expression relaxed a little. 'You've always been my very best friend,' she said. 'That's why I came here to the Lake District to find you. I didn't know what else to do, but I felt sure you would find a way to help me somehow.'

'I wish it were that simple.' Katie quickly ran her mind over all her options. 'Whatever happens, I'll have to ring them and let them know that you're safe. They weren't answering their mobiles when I tried earlier, but I've left a message for them on the answering machine at home.'

'No, they've gone into town for the day. I said I was going to be at my friend's house.'

Katie shook her head, shooting Jessica a quick glance. 'I'm amazed that you managed to find your way here at all without getting into trouble of some sort.'

'It was easy,' Jessica said, with an air of unconcern. 'I emptied my money box and went to the train station and asked for a ticket to Windermere. The man in the booth gave me a funny look, and I guessed he was a bit suspicious, so I told him I was going to visit my sister in the Lake District for the summer holidays and he said, "Oh, I see."'

Katie frowned. 'What did you plan on doing when you arrived at my house? I was out at work and the place is locked up.'

Jessica appeared crestfallen, but only for a moment. 'I would have hung around until you came home.' She gave Katie a contrite look and said quickly, 'I won't get in the way, I promise, and it'll be cool if you let me live here with you, because I'd do everything to make things easier for you. I could tidy up and help you with meals and stuff. I know how hard you have to work and how tired you used to be after being in A and E all day, but with me around, things will be much better for you, honest.'

Katie couldn't help but smile at her sister's sincere expression. 'I'm sure you would do everything you possibly could to help out, but that isn't really what's important right now, is it? We have to think about you, and what we can do to sort out your problems. It isn't just a question of you coming to live here. There would be all sorts of arrangements to be made. How could I make sure that you would be properly looked after while I'm out at work?'

Jessica pulled in a quick breath. 'I'm old enough to look after myself.'

Katie shook her head. 'But you're not, that's the whole point. And then there's school to think about. The holidays aren't going to last for ever.'

Jessica's mouth wavered as she struggled to keep her emotions in check. 'I could go to school here, couldn't I? You have to let me stay, Katie. Please, say you will, please, please? Things will work out all right, I know they will.'

'Maybe. I left a message to say that I'd take care of you

for a few days, whatever happens. We'll talk it through properly when we get home.' Katie slowed the car to a halt as the traffic came to a standstill. 'If we ever get home… I thought we would avoid this hold-up by coming this way,' she murmured distractedly. 'It looks as though we're going to be stuck here for a while, though.'

Jessica nodded and peered out of the window at the trouble up ahead. 'It looks as though everything's more or less sorted now. They're closing the ambulance doors and getting ready to move away.' She gave Katie a sideways glance. 'You know, the man who helped me—Alex, he said his name was—took this road as well. I bet he's wishing he'd gone another way. He's still following us, just a few cars behind.'

'Yes, I'd noticed.' Katie glanced in her rear-view mirror and caught sight of the gleaming blue car slowing to a halt at a bend in the road. 'Perhaps he'll turn off before we get anywhere near Ambleside.'

It was wishful thinking, a vaguely consoling thought that she had clung on to as the journey had progressed. There was something about him that made her flustered and set her pulses racing, and it was all very disturbing. His calm, quietly perceptive manner ought to have encouraged her to feel that everything was under control, but instead he had stirred up all kinds of doubt and confusion within her.

She was left feeling unnerved and edgy, but of course that might have been as a result of all that had happened. All day long she had been active, rushing about, trying to resolve one problem after another, but now that she was stuck in traffic she was forced to be still, and it was an odd feeling. She tapped her fingers on the steering-wheel, beating out a restless rhythm.

Jessica dug her in the ribs. 'Katie, look—there are skid marks on the road, right back here. Can you see them?'

Katie followed her sister's pointing finger. 'Yes, you're right. It looks as though someone took the bend too fast, hit the barrier at the side of the road and then tried to stop further on.'

'But he must have smashed into the car up front.' Jessica's eyes widened. 'That must be one of the cars that they're loading on to the retrieval truck right now.'

'I hope the people who were hurt manage to come through this safely in the end,' Katie murmured. She tried to gauge what was happening in the distance, but Jessica was jabbing her in the ribs again.

'Something's not right—look over there, in the bushes. I can see something. Come on, we have to go and find out what's going on.' Already, Jessica had released herself from her seat belt and was pushing at the passenger door.

'Jess, come back here,' Katie called out, but her sister wasn't listening. She had jumped down onto the verge at the side of the road and now she was headed for the trees.

'I don't believe this,' Katie muttered under her breath. 'Will this nightmare never end?' She manoeuvred the car onto the grass verge so that others could pass her, and then she switched off the ignition, sliding out of the driver's seat to go in search of Jessica.

'Over here,' Jessica shouted. 'There's a man—Katie, I don't think he's breathing.'

Katie made her way through the thicket of brushwood that lined the hedgerow and saw that her sister was kneeling beside a man who was lying crumpled on his side on the meadow grass.

'I saw his shoe through a break in the hedge,' Jessica said, 'so I guessed there might be someone here. Do you think he might have been thrown out of the car?'

Katie nodded. 'It looks that way. I suppose the car door might have been flung open if it hit a post, and perhaps he wasn't strapped in.' She crouched down and was busy checking the young man for signs of life. He was in his early twenties, she guessed, and from the looks of things his jaw was broken. That would make it virtually impossible for anyone to insert an airway, and that could be disastrous, because he was already struggling for air, making strange gurgling sounds.

He wasn't responding to Katie's urgent attempts to talk to him and find out if he was aware of what was going on, and she knew that he was in a bad way. 'His pulse is rapid and faint,' Katie murmured, glancing up at Jessica, who was looking shocked and pale. 'I need to help him to breathe. Do you think you could look in the glove compartment of my car for a pen or maybe a plastic drink straw, while I do what I can to clear the obstruction in his throat? And bring me the first-aid kit from the boot?' She handed over the keys.

Jessica nodded, and hurried away. Katie was relieved.

At least if the child had something to do, it would stop her from dwelling on the awfulness of the situation.

She rummaged in her bag, spilling some of the contents out onto the grass as she hastily searched for her phone. Finding it, she called for an ambulance. If only the paramedics who had attended the accident up ahead had stayed around for a few moments longer…but they hadn't, and she had to deal with this calamity all by herself.

That thought barely had time to sink in before Jessica came back, and Katie's eyes widened when she saw that her sister wasn't alone. The man from the café was with her, his face taut with concern, a line indenting his brow. He came to kneel down beside her, so close that they were almost touching one another. Katie felt her senses swim.

'Have you managed to clear his airway?' he asked.

She gave herself a mental shake. 'Not really. I've brought his tongue forward and done what I can, but he's bleeding heavily and I can't manoeuvre him properly to resuscitate him because his jaw is broken.'

'Let me see what I can do.'

He made as though he would move her to one side but she resisted, saying quietly, 'No, thank you. I believe I'll manage.' She gave him a determined blue stare. She couldn't imagine why he thought he would know any better than she did about what needed to be done. 'I'm going to improvise an airway. There's no way he can be intubated in the usual way, even if there was any time to wait.'

He frowned, his eyes narrowing, as Jessica leaned over to hand her a plastic straw and then placed the first-aid kit down on the ground beside her.

Jessica's jaw dropped as Katie opened up the box and took out a small sharp knife. 'What are you going to do?' she asked breathlessly.

'I'm going to make a small incision in his throat and put the straw in place so that he can get air into his lungs.' She looked up at her sister. 'Perhaps you should turn away for a while. You might not want to see this.'

Jessica swallowed hard but steadfastly continued to watch what was going on. Beside her, Katie felt the man stiffen.

She sent him a quick glance. 'Maybe you should look away, too,' she said. The last thing she needed was for him to pass out through squeamishness. Anyway, it was unsettling, having him watch her every movement.

He shook his head. 'Do you know what you're doing?' His whole body was poised as though he was ready to intervene at any second. Katie could feel the warmth emanating from him, almost as though he was touching her, and her skin began to tingle in response.

'Yes, it's all right.' Her voice was husky and she cleared her throat. 'I'm a doctor.' As she spoke, she was already feeling for the thyroid cartilage, and within seconds she began to make the incision. Once she had established that she had managed to puncture the cricothyroid membrane she opened up the fissure with a finger and inserted the drinking straw a little way into the trachea. Breathing into the tube, she was relieved to see that the man's chest began to rise.

'Is he going to be all right?' Jessica's eyes were wide.

'I hope so. I think he has some broken ribs, and there may be a skull fracture, but at least he's breathing now, and we've managed to buy some time for him. We can't do much more until the paramedics get here with proper equipment.'

She eased back a fraction and saw that Alex was checking the man's pulse. 'There's a strong possibility he'll go into shock,' he said. 'We don't know for sure how long he might have been lying here. His heart rate is rapid, but the pulse is weak, and I suspect his blood pressure is way down. He must be bleeding internally.' He was already getting to his feet. 'I'll go and get my medical bag from the car. We can at least put in an IV line and try to get some initial fluids into him.'

Katie stared up at him. 'You're a doctor?'

He nodded briefly, but he was already moving away from her, and after a moment Katie released a long breath. She hadn't realised how keyed up she had been, having him so close beside her that his shoulder had almost brushed against hers. It had been like being surrounded by an electric force field strong enough to make the air crackle.

She blinked. So he was a doctor, too? No wonder he had tried to intervene. She tried to absorb this new revelation and at the same time keep a check on her patient. Alex seemed to think they had met before, but surely she would have remembered him if they had been at medical school together? After all, he wasn't the kind of man you would easily forget. He was incredibly good-looking, with strong features and grey-blue eyes that seemed to penetrate deep into her soul. Just being around him had the power to stop her in her tracks.

He came back as she was taping the makeshift breathing tube securely in place. He sank down next to her on the grass and opened up his black leather case, but this time she was prepared, and with an effort she managed to keep her pulse rate under control.

'I don't carry a lot with me,' he said in an undertone, 'but I have some lactated Ringer's solution, which will help until we can get him to hospital. They talk about the golden hour, but we're fast losing ground there.'

Jessica was puzzled. 'What's the golden hour?'

Alex was attempting to find a vein, and Katie realised that it was going to be difficult if the man's circulation was shutting down.

'It's the maximum time lapse from when the trauma happened to arrival at hospital, if the patient is to stand a good chance of survival.' He slid the needle into place. 'I'm in.' Quickly he set up the IV line and hooked up the Ringer's solution, using an overhead branch to keep the bag above the level of the patient.

'At least…' Jessica's voice broke, becoming thready. 'At least he has you and Katie to look after him.'

Alex gave her a brief smile, and perhaps he realised

that she was very young and vulnerable because he said softly, 'We're doing everything we can for him.'

Jessica nodded, and watched as Alex drew up a syringe. 'What's that you're giving him?'

'It's an antibiotic. We haven't been able to use sterile equipment out here, so this should help to ward off any infection.' He sent her a thoughtful glance. 'You seem very keen to know what's going on. Are you thinking of going into medicine like your sister? I suppose she must be a great influence in your life, working as a doctor?'

Jessica gave an awkward shrug. 'I'm not sure what I want to do. I used to go and see Katie sometimes when she worked in A and E and she explained some of it to me, but she doesn't work there now, and I'm not sure I'd be able to do that kind of job. I know Katie gave it up. She doesn't work as a doctor any more, and I don't know if I'm cut out for it either.'

Alex turned his gaze on Katie, his brows meeting in a dark line. 'Is that true? You're not working in medicine now?'

Katie nodded. 'It isn't easy to find placements these days, as you probably know. Anyway I wanted a change, so I found myself a job in a rehabilitation centre. It was good. I enjoyed working there.' She grimaced wryly. 'Unfortunately, the place closed down this afternoon, so it looks as though I'll be looking through the situations vacant columns for something else first thing tomorrow.'

He opened his mouth as though to say something, but in the distance a siren sounded, growing nearer.

They both checked their patient, relieved to find that his condition was reasonably stable for the moment. Alex began to gather up the equipment they had used, closing his medical bag and handing the first-aid kit to Jessica as the ambulance arrived.

The paramedics oversaw the patient's transfer to the waiting ambulance, and Alex gave the team a rundown of the man's injuries. 'We'll need to get a CT scan and move him to Theatre as soon as possible,' he said. 'I'll follow you to the hospital and help with the handover to A and E. Martin's on duty today, isn't he?'

The paramedic nodded. 'We'll get in touch with him and tell him to stand by.'

'Good.' He stood back and waited while the men made sure their patient was securely strapped in place in the vehicle. Turning to Katie, he said, 'There's a place for you on my team if you want it. I'm in charge of the A and E department at South Lake Hospital. I've been advertising for a senior house officer for a few weeks now, and so far I haven't managed to fill the position. None of the candidates have been right for the job. If you drop by the department some time tomorrow, we could go through the application forms together.'

Was he actually offering her a job? Katie's mouth dropped open, but she quickly attempted to recover herself. 'I don't think so,' she murmured. 'I mean…thanks all the same, but I think I'll take some time and look around.'

He was frowning again. 'I don't understand why you're hesitating. Didn't you say that you were out of work and posts were hard to find?' His grey-blue eyes homed in on her with laser-like precision. 'I've seen you in action and I've no doubt that you know what you're doing. You acted promptly in an emergency and you probably brought this man back from the brink. Is there a problem of some sort, a reason why you won't consider the offer?'

She shook her head. 'There's no problem. I just prefer to give it some thought, that's all.' Her chin tilted. She didn't see why she had to lay her life bare for this man. He had dropped into her life from out of nowhere, and he could just as easily disappear into nothingness once more. Out of sight, out of mind—wasn't that what people said? And that being the case, the spectre of working in A and E once more would disappear along with him, wouldn't it?

'I can't stay and debate the matter with you,' he said on a brisk note, 'but I think you're making a mistake.' He pressed his lips together in a straight line. 'I have to go.'

He glanced at Jessica, who had gone to stand a short distance away from the ambulance, watching the paramedics make their preparations to leave. Then he turned his attention back to Katie.

'How are you going to manage? Don't you owe it to that young girl to keep a roof over her head?' His grey eyes darkened. 'Or maybe she comes a long way down on your list of priorities? I suppose that could explain a lot.'

Katie straightened her back. 'You don't know anything about me, or my sister,' she said. 'How can you presume to judge me when we've only just met?'

He inclined his head a fraction. 'That's true,' he murmured, and his mouth indented in a vestige of a smile. 'You're definitely something of an enigma, Katie Sorenson…but I dare say I'll fathom the puzzle somehow.'

He moved swiftly away from her and headed towards his car, stopping only to say a quick goodbye to Jessica. Then he slid behind the wheel and sped away in the wake of the ambulance.

Jessica came over to where Katie was standing. 'Did I hear him offer you a job?'

Katie nodded. 'Yes. He seems to think I could find a place in his A and E department, but I told him I wanted to look around for something else. That's why I moved here, so that I could put all that behind me and make a fresh start.'

Jessica nodded. 'Yes, I know, but you'll be going to work in another A and E department at some point, won't you? You have to, surely? You're a good doctor, and you're needed out there. Anyway, you weren't ever going to stay at the rehab centre for very long, were you?'

Katie started to walk towards her car. 'Actually I found that it was far more rewarding than I expected. It was certainly less frantic than what I was doing at the hospital, and I wasn't planning on making a change yet.'

'But you told Alex that you were out of work now.' Jessica shook her head, so that her glossy brown curls danced in the afternoon sunlight. 'You can't give up on being a doctor. It isn't right. Just because things went wrong for you back home. I don't care what anybody says, I know you, and I know you couldn't have done anything wrong. You're always so careful, so good in everything that you do. Everyone knows that…Mum says that's why they haven't put anything bad in your work record.' She looked at Katie. 'They haven't, have they?'

Katie bent her head a fraction, so that her chestnut curls momentarily fell across her cheek, covering her features. 'That may be so, but I still don't feel that I can work in A and E.' She frowned, her blue eyes clouding. 'I was getting on all right at the rehab centre. I liked working with the staff there, and it was good to know that I was helping people to get back on their feet after they were incapacitated.'

Jessica put her arms around her in a fleeting hug. 'I'm sorry it came to an end. You'll have to tell me what happened. But even so, it seems all wrong to me that you were working there in the first place. You used to love being in Emergency. You went through all that training, and it was all you ever wanted to do, remember? Now that I'm here, you can go back to it, can't you? And things will be easier for you because I'll be here to tidy up and make the meals, and just as soon as I find a job I'll be able to help out with the finances.'

Katie smiled. Oh, for youthful innocence. Her sister made it all sound so simple. All she had to do was go after what she wanted and things would turn out fine. It was a lovely thought, and if only that was the way things worked she would be more than happy…but there was more to it than that, wasn't there?

Her confidence had been badly shaken, and all her hopes and dreams had crumbled about her. Life would never be quite the same ever again.

'We should head back to my cottage,' Katie said, pulling open her car door. 'You can tell me what went wrong at home and why you decided to come all the way out here.'

Jessica pulled a face as she settled herself in the passenger seat. 'Do I have to? I'd much rather talk about you and Alex and the job at his hospital.' She rolled her eyes in a dramatic gesture. 'When he's not trying to take charge of me he's really something, isn't he? I bet the girls back home would think he was gorgeous.'

Katie threw her a look from under her lashes. 'That may be so, but we aren't going to see him again, so perhaps we should try to forget about him. We'll concentrate on you from now on.'

It was a brave attempt at self-protection on Katie's part—easier to forget about it and move on. Those all-seeing, grey-blue eyes were imprinted on her mind, though, and the promise that glimmered within them would haunt her for some time to come.

'Oh, phooey.' Jessica rolled her eyes. 'He's a dreamboat, and you're such a spoilsport. How can you not want to talk about him?'

# CHAPTER THREE

'SO, THIS is your place?' Jessica's grey eyes widened as she gazed at the L-shaped, stone-built cottage in front of her. 'I never imagined that you would buy anything like this. It's lovely, really quaint, and so different from our place back home.'

Katie nodded, looking up at the gabled roofs that were at angles to one another. 'I think that's because it's so open here—everything around is green and peaceful, and there aren't that many houses dotted about. You only have to look out of the bedroom window and you can see crags and fells for miles around. Mind you, once we get inside you might feel differently about it. It's quite poky, and there's still a lot that I have to do to make the place feel comfortable.'

Katie started to unlock the front door, but Jessica hung back, lightly touching the silky, pale mauve petals of the wisteria that covered the front wall. 'This is beautiful,' she murmured, breathing in the sweet fragrance.

'Yes, you're right, it is.' Katie paused to share the

moment with her sister. 'I ought to stop more often and take time to appreciate what I have.' The truth was, lately all she had thought about was how much work there was to do, and how wild and overgrown the garden had become. She gave a half-smile. Having her sister here with her was already making a difference to her outlook on things.

'Come through to the kitchen and I'll make us some tea.' She glanced at Jessica. 'You'd better put your hold-all down. It looks heavy. You must have brought every-thing with you bar the kitchen sink.'

Jessica gave an awkward laugh. 'I packed as much as I could manage.' She looked up at Katie, biting down on her lower lip.

'I know it must be awkward for you, with me turning up here like this, out of the blue, but I didn't know what else to do. I couldn't stay at home, not after the way Dad's temper took off. He locked me out of the house, and it was all because I was a few minutes late getting in. I went and spent the night round at my friend's house, but I knew I had to get away. I couldn't stand it any more, and all I could think of was that you might take me in.'

Jessica was silent for a moment, deep in thought. 'You know how he is, and I'm sure that's why you left home as soon as you could manage it. It was bad enough when you went off to medical school, but at least that was close by and you were able to come home for a few days every week. Then when you started on your house officer jobs at different hospitals, I thought I was going to lose you.'

Katie gave her sister a hug. 'Has it been so bad? I'm sorry if you felt that I was leaving you behind. You know I was always there for you, just a short car ride away. I kept in touch and came to see you as often as I could.'

'Yes, and that was good, but now you've moved up here to the Lake District, and it isn't as though you could just drop by every weekend, is it? I just didn't think I could go on this way any longer. Dad's always going on at me about something or other. He says I'm scatterbrained and I'll always be troublesome.'

'Have you tried talking to Mum about how you feel?'

'What would be the point in doing that?' Jessica made a hopeless gesture with her hands. 'Mum never listens, and she certainly never takes my side. She just says, "Oh, I can't cope with the two of you arguing all the time. You're making my head hurt." She always seems as though everything's too much for her and I think she'll be better off with me out of the way.'

'You know that's not true. She loves you.' Even so, Katie had to acknowledge that her mother had never coped well with any form of stress, and it wasn't hard for her to imagine what Jessica was going through.

She washed her hands at the sink and started to prepare a light meal for the two of them, but all the time she was busy turning over all the options in her mind. It was a difficult situation, but she couldn't help feeling that her sister needed a breathing space, time to gather up her defences and allow her to face up to the world once more.

'You can stay here for a few days at least,' she told her, 'maybe even a couple of weeks, while we work out what we're going to do. I'll do what I can to square things with Mum and Dad.'

She knew it wasn't quite what Jessica had been hoping for, but the girl nodded and gave her a relieved smile. 'Thanks, Katie. I'll show you how good I can be, and then perhaps you'll let me stay for longer.' Her gaze was pleading and Katie hugged her once more.

'We'll see,' she said. 'I'll show you where the second bedroom is and, if you like, you can put your things away in there while I finish making supper.'

An hour or so later, they were sitting down to eat at the kitchen table when the doorbell rang. Katie frowned. 'I can't think who that would be,' she murmured, getting to her feet. 'You go on with your meal,' she told Jessica, who stood up as though to go with her.

'It wouldn't be Mum or Dad, would it?' Jessica's expression was apprehensive. 'You said they agreed to let me stay when they rang back earlier. Do you think they might have changed their minds?'

'I don't know, but if it is them, I'll sort it out, don't worry.'

When she opened the front door, though, she was startled to see the man who was standing in her porch. He was gazing around at the old stonework and casting a glance over the rough stone wall that edged the property.

'Alex?' She stared at him. 'What are you doing here? How did you find me?' He had changed out of the business suit and now he was wearing casual clothes, dark trousers and a jacket that was open to reveal a cool cotton shirt in a shade of blue-grey that matched his eyes. She dragged her gaze away from his rangy body and looked up at him once more, trying to cover her discomfiture.

'I asked Jessica for your address when we were at the café. I wanted to make sure that I was making a safe handover.'

Katie frowned. 'Is that why you're here? Do you think I might be mistreating her in some way?' Even the thought that he might doubt her in some way was enough to bring an affronted glare to her blue eyes.

His mouth twisted in the semblance of a smile. 'Are you always this touchy?' He looked her over as though she might give him a resounding agreement to that statement, and her eyes narrowed on him.

'Not usually.' She sighed and stood back, waving him into the cramped hallway. 'I'm having a bad day.' Running a hand through the tangle of her long, chestnut curls, she indicated the far door, which led into the kitchen. 'Come in, won't you? I apologise for my bad manners. I'm really not myself today.'

'Thanks.' He stepped inside the house and looked around, taking in the low ceiling and the narrow passageway. Katie hoped he hadn't noticed the spot in the far corner where the paint was peeling from the wall. Through a doorway to one side of the hall the living room was visible, and it was possible to glimpse from there the overgrown garden through the French doors. 'This is cosy,' he murmured. 'Have you lived here for long?'

'Um…a couple of months. I'm still decorating and trying to make the place my own, but I've been busy and I've had to make choices about where to start.'

He nodded. 'I guess it isn't easy when you're working.' He gave her a sideways glance. 'Though by all accounts that won't be much of a problem from now on, will it?'

Katie gave a shrug. 'I've already had a quick skim through the job vacancy columns in the newspaper. Apparently they need someone in the rehab unit at the local hospital. That would be a start, I suppose.'

'But it would also be a complete waste of your talents. You're a doctor. You should be using the medical skills you acquired after all those years of training.'

Perhaps he had a point there, but Katie wasn't in the mood to be judged and found wanting. She stiffened. 'I don't see why that should concern you.' She pushed open the kitchen door and ushered him through.

Jessica was sitting at the table at the far end of the room, her fork poised in her hand, but she laid it down on her plate and blinked as Alex walked into the room.

'Alex?' Her face lit up in a shy smile. 'You found me? I didn't think we would see you again so soon.'

'No, it is sooner than expected, I must agree with you there. I'm glad that you seem to have settled back in here without too much upset.' He sent a quick glance around the room. 'It's homely in here, very clean and cheerful.'

Katie had placed a bowl of roses on the worktop, and

she had set out groups of fine glassware and ceramics at intervals on shelves around the room. It wasn't much, but it made the difference between what might have been purely a functional kitchen and what she considered to be the heart of the home. What had he been expecting, something austere and unwelcoming?

She sent him a dark, cynical glance. 'See? She's perfectly well. I haven't locked her in a cupboard or banished her to bed without so much as a bowl of gruel, if that's what you were thinking.' Her mouth made a derisive slant. 'Are you satisfied now that you've seen for yourself that she's all right?'

He turned, his grey-blue gaze homing in on her. 'Actually, that isn't the reason I'm here.'

'Oh.' Katie swallowed hard. Perhaps riling him wasn't such a good idea after all. He had done nothing but help out today, and she was beginning to sound like an ungrateful harridan. That wasn't at all like her, and she couldn't for an instant fathom why he should be having this effect on her. Perhaps this awful day was beginning to get to her. She said slowly, 'It wasn't?'

He shook his head and reached inside his jacket pocket. 'When I cleared up the equipment after we had helped the man by the roadside, I must have accidentally scooped up your notebooks. I found this when I restocked my medical bag. There are some addresses and phone numbers in there, and I thought perhaps you might need it.' He handed over the small leather case.

'Oh, I…uh… Thank you.' Katie tried to accept it with good grace. 'It must have dropped out of my bag when I was looking for my phone. I thought I had put everything back.' He was wrong-footing her at every turn, and she found herself wishing for all the world that she could rewind the day and start over again. Maybe she would do things differently, given the chance.

She flicked through the pages of the small notebook. 'I'm so glad that you brought this back to me. I would have been lost without it.'

'You're welcome.' He nodded to Jessica and then turned, as though he was getting ready to leave, causing Jessica to raise her brows behind his back and gesticulate wildly to Katie as though she was wrong to let him escape. When Katie didn't react, Jessica shook her head, and obviously thought she was a hopeless case.

Katie frowned. Then, just in time, she recovered herself and said quickly, 'Do you have to go right now? I think Jess would be glad of the chance to talk to you for a while, and there's some tea in the pot. You could help yourself to some supper, too, if you like. There's plenty left.' She drifted a hand over the tabletop. 'I made too much pizza, and there's plenty of salad, if you would like some. Please, sit down and help yourself. I expect you've been too busy these last few hours to think about food.'

He seemed to hesitate, but only for a moment. 'Thank you,' he said. 'I must say it's been a while since I've eaten, and this does look good.' He pulled out a chair and sat down, then frowned at the triangular segments of the pizza. 'Did you really make this yourself?'

Did he have to doubt everything about her? Katie

bit back a withering retort and managed to send him a sweet smile instead. 'Yes, I did. It isn't all that difficult, you know.'

He bit off a corner section, savouring the combined flavours of melted cheese, tomato and herbs, and gave her a quizzical look in return. Perhaps he had decided to ignore the underlying thread of sarcasm in her voice, because he concentrated instead on finishing off his food while parrying questions from Jessica.

He circumvented the more personal queries, but answered others. She wanted to know what exactly he did at the hospital, and what his meeting would have been about if he had managed to get to it in time.

'I'm in charge of the A and E department at South Lake,' he told her. 'I started off there as a registrar, but now I've moved up the ladder and I'm a consultant. I'd like to progress even further, and perhaps take charge of a bigger unit, but that all depends on how I get on in this post. I have to go to lots of meetings so that I can keep in touch with what's going on in other hospitals in the area.'

Jessica was enthralled and, considering that she had been his reluctant detainee earlier, that said something about the man's charisma.

Katie poured tea and handed him a cup. 'How is the man we found at the side of the road doing? Have they managed to stabilise his condition?' She chose her words carefully, because she didn't want to upset Jessica in any way, and perhaps he realised that, as he answered in a fairly guarded manner.

'When I left, they were taking him along to Intensive Care. They found the source of his internal injuries and he went to Theatre to have that put right. It's going to be a question of time now more than anything. Time for him to heal, and for the swelling around his brain to ease.'

Katie's gaze was troubled. It didn't sound too good, but at least she felt that they had done all they could for the man. 'I dread to think what would have happened if we had just driven past him. It's all because of Jessica that we stopped to investigate in the first place.'

He nodded. 'You did really well,' he said, giving the young girl an encouraging smile. It was a smile that lit up his face and gave Katie a glimpse of features that she had not noticed before now. His mouth was perfectly formed, she saw, his teeth were straight and gleaming like pearls, and his eyes were pure heaven, filled with dancing lights that would have sparked any woman's dreams to flame.

She brought herself back to reality with a jerk. What was she thinking? How could she allow herself to even contemplate falling for any man, let alone this one? He was nothing if not sceptical of her, and here she was, slipping into a well of elusive imaginings about him. What was wrong with her? Emotions, especially those between men and women, from her experience, were fragile things, as light and insubstantial as mist. Trust in them and you could be hurt. She had to get a grip.

'I have to go,' he said, wiping his fingers on a paper serviette and unfolding himself from his chair. 'It's getting late and there's still a lot I have to do before morning.' He said goodbye to Jessica, who beamed him a smile in return.

'I'll see you out,' Katie murmured. Her pulses were pounding and she had a fight on her hands to bring them under control. This was madness. She didn't even like the man. She didn't know him, for heaven's sake, so why on earth was she getting herself into a fever over him?

'Thanks for the supper. It was delicious, and exactly what I needed.'

'It was the least I could do. Thank you for returning my notebook.'

They walked out into the hallway and he stopped at the door and looked directly into her eyes. 'Will you reconsider coming to work with me?'

She shook her head. 'No… I'm sorry, but I can't. I need a break from medicine. It's too frantic, too harrowing. I don't want to go there.'

He looked at her oddly. 'I think you're making a big mistake. Whatever it was that made you doubt yourself, you need to get back in there. Face up to your demons and stop them from getting the upper hand.'

'I don't have any demons. I just need a change.' What did he know about it? Facing up to the traumas of the past was much easier said than done, wasn't it? She saw him to the door. 'Goodbye, Alex,' she murmured.

'Goodbye?' He gave her a slight smile. 'We'll see.' He inclined his head to her and then went out of the door, walking briskly along the path to where he had parked his car at the roadside.

Katie's brow furrowed. We'll see? What was that supposed to mean?

Over the week that followed, she spent time with Jessica and did what she could to help her sister forget the problems at home. She signed her up for supervised activity sessions so that she would be able to mix with people of her own age.

Was she doing the right thing? At the back of her mind she knew that she couldn't allow the situation to drift for ever. There were decisions to be made, and above all she had to find herself a job.

'Are you going to try for the post in rehab?' Jessica asked as they were clearing up the breakfast dishes one morning. 'You said you were comfortable with that kind of work, didn't you?'

Katie nodded. 'I have an interview lined up for later on this morning at the hospital. I'll drop you off at the arts and crafts centre and pick you up on my way home.'

'OK.' Jessica seemed happy enough with the arrangement, and Katie was glad about that because it made her more settled in her mind about leaving her.

At the hospital, though, the job she was applying for wasn't exactly what she had envisaged.

'We should have said in the advertisement that it was only part time,' the woman who headed up the unit advised her. 'Sorry, but there was a problem at the printers, and the hours weren't stated correctly when the advert went out. It would actually be just a couple of hours a day, and it wouldn't involve any kind of therapeutic involvement with the patients. It's more to do with assessing the welfare of the individual and sorting out any problems they might be having during their stay with us.'

Katie tried not to show her disappointment. It was proving more difficult than she had envisaged to find work that would be satisfying and at the same time enable her to keep up with the mortgage repayments. This was a blow, but she wasn't quite ready to throw in the towel yet. Maybe something would turn up.

In the meantime, as she was already at the hospital, she could at least go and ask after the man from the road accident.

'He's out of Intensive Care,' the desk clerk told her, 'but they've transferred him to a side ward so that he can be monitored for a week or so.'

Katie made her way to the ward, not knowing quite what to expect. Perhaps she would simply introduce herself, check that he was getting along all right, and then leave.

'I thought you might be coming along to see our patient.' A familiar, deep voice sounded in her ear just as she was hesitating at the door to the ward, and she turned to see Alex coming towards her from the nurses' station. 'He's doing fine. There was some damage to his spleen, along with everything else, but they operated, and now he's recovering well.'

Katie stared at him, the breath catching in her lungs. 'You were expecting me?'

He nodded. 'I knew that the rehab interviews were taking place today, and I guessed that you might come along here afterwards.'

'I might not have given it a thought.'

He shook his head. 'You saved his life, and then you rang the hospital afterwards to see how he was doing. The nurses told me that you had been enquiring after him. I knew that you wouldn't be satisfied until you heard that he was properly on the mend.'

Her brows lifted. 'You seem to know more about me than I do myself.'

He gave a faint chuckle. 'Not really, but I just have this feeling that your emotions run deep. There's a lot you keep hidden, and that makes you hard to read, but I dare say I'll get there one of these days.'

'I can't think why you would want to bother.' She frowned. 'Aren't we simply ships that pass in the night?'

He was thoughtful for a moment, his eyes darkening. 'I don't believe that. We've met somewhere before, you and I, I'm sure of it. I just can't quite put my finger on the time and place. The name Sorenson doesn't ring a bell either, but I've no doubt I'll work it out at some point.'

His glance drifted over her, taking in the neatly tailored suit she was wearing, the skirt that clung faithfully to her hips and the jacket that nipped in at her narrow waist. His gaze shimmered over her long legs and the stilettos that complemented the outfit, before coming back to her face. 'You'd have thought it was impossible for me to forget someone who looks the way you do… beautiful copper-coloured hair, eyes like jewels, a perfect figure.' He gave his head a shake as though to clear it. 'It'll come back to me.'

Katie's mouth had dropped open, but now she clamped it shut. Did he really think she looked good? Why did that matter to her? Even so, she couldn't suppress the warm ripple of pleasure that ran through her at his words. Except for that last remark, because, like him, she still had the feeling that they had met somewhere before. But where?

She cast the thought from her mind. 'Perhaps I should get on. Were you on your way to see the patient? I don't want to intrude in any way.'

'We'll go in and see him together, if you like.'

She nodded. It would probably be easier with both of them visiting. They were all strangers to one another, with one common link—the accident.

'I'm glad you're both here,' Matt Johnson said once introductions had been made. He was sitting up in bed, looking very different from how he had appeared just over a week ago. His eyes were bright and alert, and he had colour in his cheeks. 'I wanted to thank you for everything that you did for me. They told me I might have died if it hadn't been for you two. I'm really very grateful to you both.'

'It's my little sister who deserves all the credit. She was the one who spotted you lying there.' Katie smiled at him. 'It's good to see you sitting up and talking.' His jaw had been broken, but he was managing to make himself understood, and clearly he was going to make a good recovery.

They left him in good spirits a few minutes later, and when they were out in the corridor Alex led Katie towards the lift. He said quietly, 'How did the interview go, by the way? Did they take you on?'

Katie shook her head. 'It wasn't right for me. I understood that it was to be a full-time position, but it turns out that it's only part time. That won't do for me.' She sighed. 'I'll just have to keep on looking.'

'I'm sorry. I didn't think it would be what you wanted.' He was silent for a moment and then said, 'Would you like to come and see our A and E department while you're here? I can give you a whistle-stop tour. It isn't particularly large, but generally the staff are a friendly crew, and I think you'll be taken with the great atmosphere in the unit.'

'It sounds as though you're trying to sell it to me.' She gave him a wry look. 'I told you I don't want to work in A and E.'

'I realise that, but it wouldn't hurt to take a look around, would it?'

By now they had arrived at the lift, and she decided she may as well go along with him. It was easier to do that than to stand here and argue with him.

'I suppose so.'

His mouth made a satisfied quirk. 'That's good.' They stepped into the lift and he pushed the button for the ground floor. 'I would have thought it was difficult for you to take proper care of your sister if you don't have a job to go to. Teenagers don't come cheap these days, and it must cause all kinds of problems for you.' He gave her a sideways glance. 'Of course, you might have independent means, for all I know.'

Katie's eyes flashed a warning. 'Will you stop with the persuasive tactics? I can sort my own problems out.'

He leaned a hand up against the wall of the lift. 'Can you? How's Jessica doing? Has she managed to get over whatever it was that made her want to leave home? Since I've met you, I can't imagine that it was any more than teenage hormones and a slight difference of opinion between you.'

Katie pressed her lips together in an awkward shape. 'I think I should come clean with you over that,' she murmured. 'Jess wasn't leaving me. The truth is, she ran away from our parents' home, and she was trying to find me all along. She didn't want to tell you because she thought you would put her back on the train.'

He stared at her. 'She was probably right. I certainly would have tried to make contact with her parents.' The lift came to a stop and the doors opened. 'What on earth are you doing, taking care of her?' he asked as they stepped out into the corridor. 'Are you going to send her home?'

'She's my sister. Why wouldn't I take care of her? And, no, I don't think I'll be sending her home for a while. There are too many issues to be resolved before I can do that.' She frowned. 'Anyway, what's caused this sudden about-turn? Not so long ago, you were criticising me for *not* doing my duty.'

'That was when I believed she was your responsibility. You must be mad to even think about taking on the care of a young girl when you don't need to. Don't you have enough to contend with already?'

'With losing my job, you mean?' She shook her head. 'That's nothing compared with what Jessica has been going through, but, then, I dare say you have next to no idea about what it's like to be part of a dysfunctional family. You probably had your parents behind you every step of the way, helping you through medical school and supporting you through every challenge. What do you know about family breakdown?'

'Believe me, I wouldn't let it hamper me if there was something I wanted to achieve.'

By now they had reached the double doors that led into the A and E unit, and he walked with her into the department, his stride long and brisk. She sent him an oblique glance and saw that his jaw was rigid, his eyes taking on a determined glitter.

No, he wouldn't let anything stand in his way, would he? He was a man who would succeed no matter what, because he had something inside him that would set him on the right path and keep him there.

Hadn't she met someone like him before, someone who had toughed it out no matter what the circumstances, and had made it his aim to live life to the full?

He stopped suddenly and turned to face her, his eyes widening, and she drew in a quick breath as realisation hit her.

'It was the children's home, wasn't it?' she said in a breathless whisper. 'That was where we met, all those years ago. You were just a boy, just a couple of years older than Jess is now. They called you Al, and sometimes they were cruel, in the way children are occasionally, because your parents had problems and you could never rely on them to be there for you.'

'And you were Katie Metcalf. You were there because your father died and your mother was going through a nervous breakdown.' His features had taken on an arrested expression. 'Lord, how many years ago was that? I still remember that quiet little waif who would shut herself away from everyone else and disappear for hours at a time.'

She remembered him, too. Tall and good-looking even then, he had been the focus of all the girls' attention. They had fought over him and he had laughed it off and teased them.

It had been as though he had been impervious to pain. He had shrugged it off and toughed it out, all swagger and bravado, and she had kept her distance because she had recognised even then that he had the power to break her heart.

# CHAPTER FOUR

THE doors to the A and E department swished open and Alex laid a hand in the small of Katie's back, gently urging her into the department. His touch was light and fleeting, but even so it heightened all her senses and sent the blood racing through her veins.

'No wonder I felt that I knew you from somewhere,' he murmured. 'We must have been at the children's home together for several months before you left to go back to live with your mother.'

'I couldn't place you either,' she murmured, 'but, then, you've changed. I can't quite put my finger on it, but your features are somehow different from when you were younger.' Perhaps it was that his face had matured, the bone structure was more defined, and he had lost that lean and hungry look. His hair was still jet black, but it was expertly cut and shaped now, a far cry from the tousled mane he'd had as a child.

'You've changed, too. You were always pretty, but now…now you're beautiful… And your hair was never this long or this glorious explosion of curls.' He smiled. 'You always pinned it back as though it had to be brought under control by whatever means possible.'

Alex let his gaze wander over her, and she hoped that he couldn't see the warm flush that must be colouring her cheeks. 'I remember that you weren't like the other girls who were staying there with us,' he said. 'Most of the time you were quiet and reserved, as though you were in a world of your own. But it was a different matter if some poor soul was being picked on…you were there like a shot, ready to defend him or her.'

He gave a half-smile. 'I realised then that there was a fire burning deep inside you. There was a lot more to you than met the eye.'

Katie wrinkled her nose. 'We all had our own private sorrows. Some people handled them better than others, I suppose. I was grieving for my father and sad for my mother, and I didn't feel as though I could take part in the general banter and rough and tumble. My parents had been divorced, but they still kept in touch, and I saw my father on a regular basis.' She gave him a wry smile. 'I envied the rest of you. You all seemed to take things in your stride, though of course I know now that outward appearances don't count for much in that kind of situation.'

'That's probably true. Most of the kids hung around together and managed to muddle through somehow without too many ill effects.' His mouth twisted. 'You were different somehow. There must have been umpteen times when the house parents sent me to look for you after you went off and disappeared into the wilderness. I suppose they knew that I would find all your favourite hideaways…like the little copse down by the brook, or the fisherman's hut at the far end of the marina. We weren't supposed to go there, but those kind of rules didn't seem to bother you overmuch at that time.'

Her blue eyes softened at the memory. 'They didn't seem to worry you either. Thanks for not telling on me.' Her lips made an odd twist. 'It wasn't that I didn't want to know anybody. It was just that I needed to be alone to think things through and try to get my head straight.'

'I realised that.'

She nodded. It had been Alex above anyone else who had helped her to get through those despairing months. He had talked to her and tried to draw her out, and it hadn't been long before it had come to her that she had fallen for him, big time. Most likely it had simply been a youthful crush, but even then she had realised that he was someone she could lean on, who would lead her back to a safe haven come what may, and she had found that she longed for the moments when he would be by her side.

Only it soon dawned on her that his attention wasn't reserved for her alone. Far from it… He had been a hit with all the girls, and the boys had wanted him on their team, whatever game they had been into at the time. Alex had been devil-may-care, full of ideas about what to do, and everyone had wanted to be with him.

'Alex—uh…Dr Brooklyn, we've a patient coming in

by ambulance. Aged 30, with chest pain and shortness of breath.' A fair-haired nurse came over to Alex and handed him a clipboard. Katie guessed she had added the 'Dr Brooklyn' for her benefit.

'Ten minutes and he should be here,' the girl added. 'I've asked Colin to oversee him. Is that all right? I know you wanted him to fill in for an hour or so.'

'That's fine, Sarah.'

'Good. Will you sign these forms for me? Martin's on a lunch-break and I need to get them sent off to the lab.'

'OK.' Alex obliged, checking each of the forms before adding his bold, flowing signature. 'I've brought Katie here to show her around the department. We used to live in the same town by the Humber River, years ago. She's a doctor, and I'm hoping we can persuade her to join us as an experienced senior house officer. She's a bit reluctant, so maybe we should show her that we're all just normal, friendly people who will do our best to make her welcome.'

Sarah's expression brightened. 'An SHO? Rope her in, quick, and don't let her get away.' She smiled at Katie. 'We're desperate for doctors in here. The department has been expanding quickly, and there are far more patients than we can decently cope with. You'll love working here, I promise.'

'I'm sure it's a great unit,' Katie said softly. 'I'm just not certain that I want to work in A and E.' It was easier to put it that way than to say she couldn't cope with any kind of work as a doctor.

'Oh, Alex is a dream to work with. You'll see.' Sarah was already turning away. 'Must go. I have a dozen or more patients waiting.'

'Don't let the workload put you off,' Alex said. 'We're all very supportive of one another.'

'Maybe, but I think I'll go on looking for something else, all the same.'

His mouth took on a serious slant. 'Are you still running away, even after all these years? I thought you had more backbone than that.'

'I never ran away.' Katie looked him straight in the eye. 'I told you…I needed time to work things out back then. I had to sort it all out in my head. I wasn't like you…I didn't know how to put my past life behind me and move on.'

'What makes you think that I did?'

Her glance flickered over him. 'You were always strong and in control of yourself. People went to you with their worries and you helped them out. You always seemed to have the answers.'

'But not with you. You were the exception, weren't you? You always kept something back, just as you're doing now. I wasn't shrewd enough then to know how to reach you, and you slipped away.'

'We all moved on eventually. Look at you. Here you are, the head of a department, and you're still in your early thirties. I always knew you were a go-getter, that you wouldn't let anything stop you from climbing the mountain.' She gave a brief smile. 'Come to think of it, you always said you wanted to come to live in the Lake

District, so that's another ambition to be crossed off the list.' If he didn't have any family to leave behind, there was nothing to stand in his way. He was a free agent and could go wherever he wanted.

She looked around the unit, taking in the calm atmosphere, the quiet way in which the doctors and nurses went about their business. 'You say you have staffing problems, but you seem to have everything well in hand here.'

'It's an illusion, all smoke and mirrors.' His expression was rueful as he followed the direction of her gaze. 'You should see us on a weekend when the pubs and clubs spill out their customers. Besides, it may look quiet, but the board is filled with the names of patients being attended to.'

He took her over to the central desk and swivelled the computer monitor around so that she could see the triage screen. 'See, there are fracture patients, head injuries, suspected septicaemia—you name it, they're all there.'

'Shouldn't you be dealing with some of them?'

He inclined his head a fraction. 'Officially, I'm still off duty for the next couple of hours. Besides, I wanted to take the opportunity to learn a little more about you. And now that I've finally remembered where it was that we met, I'm all the more intrigued. What happened to you after you left the children's home? Presumably your mother must have married again? I imagine that's why I didn't recognise the name Sorenson.'

'She did. I kept the Metcalf part of my name and added Sorenson.'

'And Jessica is your half-sister?'

'That's right.'

He leaned his hip against a small side table, so that he was half sitting, half standing, and Katie's gaze was drawn to the way the fabric of his trousers was stretched across the taut expanse of his thigh. He was strong and muscular, fit and vital in a way that made her heart begin to pound. She looked away.

'So why have things suddenly gone wrong? Why can't your mother and stepfather take care of her?' Alex probed. 'Why should you be landed with all the difficulties of looking after a wayward teenager?' A siren sounded in the distance, but he took no notice and stayed where he was.

Katie frowned. 'What makes you think there are difficulties…and why do you call her wayward? You hardly know her.'

'She has to be wayward to run away in the first place. And teenagers are always trouble. They stay out late, they have issues over clothes and spending money, they get in with bad crowds.'

'Some do, perhaps, but that doesn't mean that Jess is like that. Anyway, she's young and vulnerable and I want to do my best for her. She hasn't had an easy life.'

'She's still her parents' responsibility.'

'They're going through a bad patch.' It was one that had lasted for more than a few years, but she wasn't going to tell him that. 'Mum doesn't handle stress well. She was ill and went into hospital when Jess was just a toddler, and we both ended up in care because my stepfather couldn't handle looking after both of us. I think my sister deserves a break. She's had a troubled childhood.'

'So did you, from the sound of things. You went into care at least twice. I still don't see why you have to take up their load.'

'Then it's just as well that you're not the one who has to make the decision, isn't it?' She sent him a cool stare, and he responded by batting it away as though it was of no consequence.

'The ambulance has arrived. Come and see how we work here.'

'Are you sure it's all right for me to do that?'

'Of course. Anyway, after the way you did that crike airway on Matt Johnson I looked up your registration. I wanted to be sure that you were qualified before I went ahead and drew up application forms for you to sign.'

She pulled in a quick breath. 'Don't you think you might have been getting a little ahead of yourself?'

'Yes, maybe.' He didn't seem at all concerned by her rebuke. 'Come on. The paramedics will be bringing the patient in at any moment. Colin's our registrar. He'll be handling this case.'

Katie recognised the paramedic from the previous week. 'This is Luke Hathaway,' he said, 'aged 30, complaining of chest pain radiating to both arms, shortness of breath and palpitations. There's tenderness over the anterior part of his chest wall.'

Colin supervised Luke's transfer to a resuscitation room. The registrar was a lanky individual, in his early forties, Katie guessed, and he didn't seem to mind at all when Alex asked if they could stand in on his assessment of the patient. After acknowledging her and Alex briefly, he concentrated on the young man.

He began to examine Luke's chest with a stethoscope. 'How long have you had this pain?' he asked him.

'A couple of days, on and off.' Luke struggled to get his breath. 'But it started to get worse about an hour ago.'

'Any cough?'

Luke nodded. 'I have been coughing, but it's a hard, tight cough.'

'OK. Are you on any medication, or do you use any kind of drugs?'

'No.' Luke lowered his head, frowning.

Colin studied the chart that the paramedic had handed to him. 'It says here that your father suffers from coronary artery disease, is that right?'

'Yes.'

'All right. Well, we'll do an X-ray and obtain an ECG so that we can look at the activity of your heart,' Colin told him. 'It's probably nothing serious, but we'll do some tests and check for any sign of chest infection.'

'We'll leave you to get those tests done,' Alex said, giving Luke a brief smile. 'We'll come back and look in on you later, if we may?'

Luke nodded, and Alex turned to Katie. 'I'll give you a tour around the unit,' he murmured.

He showed her the resuscitation bays first of all. 'The building is old and poky, but I arranged for it to be brightened up with a lick of paint so that it looks light and airy, and the equipment is all up to the minute.' He pointed out the triage area and the waiting room that was filled with patients waiting to be seen.

'Don't let that put you off,' he said. 'We have a good record for waiting times here. We try to be as efficient as we possibly can.'

When the tour was complete, he led her into the doctors' lounge, and offered her a cup of coffee. 'It's good stuff,' he said. 'Sarah is keen on her coffee so she makes a brew from time to time and gets someone to make sure it's freshened up at frequent intervals. That way you can always rely on a perfect cup.'

'It's delicious,' Katie said, sipping the hot liquid and savouring the aroma. 'I could almost be tempted to work here just for the coffee alone.'

He laughed. 'So I'm making some headway at last. Wonderful. Do you want a refill?'

'Let's not get too excited.' She lifted her gaze. 'I don't often give in that easily to temptation.'

'You don't?' He started towards her as she put the cup down onto the worktop, and came to a halt just beside her. His gaze ran over her, pausing to linger momentarily on her soft, feminine curves. His smoky grey glance spoke volumes, his eyes glimmering with darting lights that tantalised and teased at the same time. 'That's a real shame. I would so like to have been able to tempt you.'

Katie was suddenly flustered by his nearness. His long body was so close to hers that they were almost touching...almost, but not quite. 'I didn't...I meant...'

'I know what you meant.' He said it with a dry smile, taking a step backwards, and Katie realised that she had been holding her breath all the time he had been near. She braced herself and tried to shake off the confusion that fogged her mind.

By the time they arrived back at the resuscitation bay, where Luke Hathaway was, Colin was getting ready to discharge his patient.

'The ECG and X-ray results are normal,' he said, 'so it's most likely that the pain you're experiencing is due to a localised inflammation. It's a problem that affects the junction where the upper ribs join with the cartilage that holds them to the breastbone.'

Luke frowned, but seemed to accept what the doctor was saying to him well enough. 'So it's nothing serious, then? I thought I was having a heart attack or something.'

'That would be most unlikely,' Colin said with a smile. 'Are you experiencing much pain right now?'

Luke shook his head.

'That's good. Anyway, the cardiac enzyme test was negative. You appear to be fit in every other way, and you're young. A heart attack is not at all what we would expect in a man of your age.' He began to write out a prescription. 'I'll get the nurse to fill this out for you. I'm giving you some anti-inflammatories, along with painkillers and a course of antibiotics to clear up any infection. You should come back to us if you have any more symptoms of chest pain.'

'Thank you.' Luke was still frowning, but as Colin

left the room he began to fasten the remainder of his shirt buttons that were still undone.

'I'll be back in a moment,' Alex said. 'I just want to go and have a word with Dr Davies about another patient.'

Katie nodded, but stayed where she was. Something about the patient's manner was bothering her, but right now she was uncertain exactly what the problem was.

'Do you have anyone here who can take you home?' she asked softly.

'No, not just at the moment,' Luke replied. 'My wife called for the ambulance, but she had to leave me here so that she could go and fetch our children from play-school. Then she needed to find someone who would look after them before she could come back to me. She said she'd get here as soon as she could.' He gave an awkward smile. 'Actually, I feel a bit silly, causing everyone all this bother. I'll probably ring her and tell her that I'll get a bus back.'

'Are you sure that you feel up to doing that?' Katie queried. 'You look a bit pale to me and you're still quite breathless.'

Luke shrugged. 'The doctor said it was just a bit of inflammation.'

'Yes. You said that your father had a history of coronary artery disease. Would you like to tell me about that?'

'Well, he was very young when he had his first heart attack, in his twenties, and then he had another one when he was in his thirties. I don't know what caused it, but perhaps diet and cholesterol played a part, or it may have been that there was a weakness there from the start.'

'Hmm…that's possible, I suppose,' Katie said. 'I noticed that you were a little guarded when the doctor asked you about drug use. It's not that we would be passing judgement on you in any way, but use of certain drugs can cause problems with the heart. That's why it's important to tell us the truth so that we have all the details to hand.'

He looked uncomfortable. 'Well, perhaps I was wrong to say I didn't ever use them. I did do some cocaine last week, but that's just between you and me. I wouldn't admit to it if the police were to get involved.'

Katie nodded. 'I understand. Just remember that some drugs can be very harmful to you…and as the doctor said, if you have any more chest pain you should come back to the hospital right away.'

She looked up as she heard a movement on the other side of the room. Alex was standing in the doorway, and she wondered just how long he had been there. Had he heard any part of their conversation?

She stood up. 'I'll leave you to finish dressing,' she murmured, glancing at Luke, 'but I think you would be wise to wait here until your wife arrives. I don't believe you should attempt to go home on your own.'

Luke gave her a brief, strained smile and started to look around for his jacket.

Katie stood up and went to leave the room, meeting Alex in the doorway. He walked into the main thoroughfare of A and E with her.

'You seem to be preoccupied,' he said. 'Is something wrong? I didn't hear everything that was said, but judging by some of your questions I'm wondering if you have some doubts about whether or not the patient should be discharged.'

Katie made an awkward gesture with her shoulders. 'It isn't really for me to say, is it? I don't have any right to interfere. I don't even work here.'

'But…?' Alex was studying her thoughtfully.

She grimaced. He wasn't going to leave it alone, was he? 'I wouldn't be so sure that he isn't suffering from some sort of impending heart problem. He confided to me that he used cocaine, and together with the fact that his father suffered from cardiac problems at a young age, I would be inclined to keep him here under observation for a while longer. I would also order up further cardiac enzyme tests.'

'Yes, I'd been considering that, too, and I think you're probably right. I'll suggest that course of action to Dr Davies.'

Katie was faintly alarmed. 'I don't want him to feel that I'm intruding. After all, it isn't really any of my business, but he's bound to know that the impetus came from me, surely?'

'That won't matter. The patient wasn't fully truthful with him from the outset, and we didn't know the extent of the family history. I don't think Dr Davies will take it amiss.'

Katie wasn't too sure about that, but Alex was already moving in Colin's direction. 'Do you have a moment, Colin?' she heard him ask.

She almost wished that she could have disappeared through a hole in the floor. No doctor wanted someone else telling him that he was making a mistake in letting a patient go. It undermined his authority and brought his competence into question. Her only hope was that she would somehow be able to smooth things over.

Colin was frowning, but a few moments later he passed by her on his way to the resuscitation bay. 'I hear that our patient wasn't fully open with me about his background,' he said briskly. 'Of course, that puts a different slant on things. I'm going to suggest that he stays here overnight, so that we can keep an eye on him.'

'That's probably a good idea,' Kate murmured. She hesitated before adding, 'I hope you don't think that I was intruding. It was only that I stayed to talk to the patient for a while, otherwise we would have had no idea that there was a problem.'

Colin's face was impassive. 'As you say, we didn't get the full picture.' He was polite and clearly ready to do the right thing, but she couldn't read him at all. A chill went through her. Had she made an enemy?

'Katie,' Alex said, coming back to her and drawing her to one side, 'I have to go on duty in a while, but I wanted to make one last effort to persuade you to think again about the job. Do you think you could give some more thought to joining our team? I would have to make some checks, of course, references from your last hospital post and so on, but I can't see that there would be any problems, and we could take you on almost immediately. It's all down to whether you could handle being in

Emergency again, but I would be here to back you up at every stage.'

He led her into a side room. Looking around, she saw that it was an office, and she guessed that it belonged to him. It was neat, the desktop highly polished, with papers stacked neatly in a wire tray and notes pinned up on a corkboard on the wall. Sunlight streamed in through a large window.

'You would be perfect for this job,' he said. 'You've proved that to me more than once in the last few days. You can't spend your life running away from difficult situations and hiding yourself in quiet corners, you know. I won't let you, especially now that I've found you again after all this time. It feels as though fate has brought us back together. That has to mean something, doesn't it?'

Katie's blue eyes were troubled. Was she really running away? It made her seem like such a coward, but she had never thought of herself that way. Life had dealt her a blow and her way of coming to terms with the destruction of her career had been to retreat to lick her wounds.

She looked at him. He was right, wasn't he? He was offering her the chance to put her toe back in the water, and perhaps that was what she must do if she was ever to get her confidence back.

'All right. I'll do it.' She pulled in a deep breath. 'I don't know how it's going to work out, but I'll do my best.'

'That's brilliant.' He came over to her and put his arms around her, hugging her close, so that the heat of his body permeated the soft fabric of her suit and brought warmth to every part of her. 'I knew you couldn't let this chance pass you by. This position is tailor-made for you, and I'll be here with you to see you through, every step of the way. It's great, Katie. It's going to work out, you'll see.'

Katie couldn't think straight. The way he was holding her was causing a meltdown in her head, and all she could think of was that her breasts were crushed against the solid wall of his chest and her legs were pressed up against the taut length of his thighs. It took her breath away, this closeness, and made her head spin as though she was caught up in a whirlwind that caused her senses to spiral out of control.

She was already regretting her decision. How was she going to be able to work with him? Wasn't this the way it had always been? Years ago, he would find her wherever she was hiding and he would coax her back into facing the world once more, and for a while everything would go well. It was the turning point that came afterwards that she dreaded. The moment when she knew that his hugs were not for her alone, and the world was still a cruel place in which to live.

'Let's go and get those papers signed,' he murmured, reluctantly drawing away from her, and it must have been that she was still caught up in the heat of the moment because while her head was still full of cotton-wool clouds she found herself signing on the dotted line, and after that her future was sealed. There was no going back.

## CHAPTER FIVE

'SO, HOW are you settling into the new job?' Nathan, Katie's neighbour, was sitting at the breakfast table in the kitchen, munching a slice of crispy toast. 'You were worried about taking on any kind of work that had to do with practising medicine, weren't you?'

'I was,' Katie said with a frown. 'I still am, not just because of the type of work but because I'm anxious in case there are any repercussions from what happened at my old hospital. I wasn't even sure whether my former boss would give me a reference, but things seem to have turned out all right in the end. He wrote a brief account of my work in A and E and didn't make any mention of the problem I had when I was carrying out that surgery.'

She was pouring tea from an earthenware pot, and now she handed a cup to Jessica, who was sitting at the other side of the table. The teenager was scanning the picture puzzle on the back of a cereal box, away in a world of her own.

'So far I think I'm handling everything all right,' Katie added. 'There was a patient who was being discharged when I was looking around the unit, and I felt that he needed to be admitted for observation. It was just as well that they kept him in because apparently he had a heart attack a few hours later, and luckily a medical team was on hand to tend to him, so he's going to be all right. That made me feel a bit better about trusting my own judgement. It's just a question of getting used to the fast pace again.'

There was also the matter of adjusting to the fact that she was in close proximity with Alex every day, but she wasn't going to confide in Nathan about that.

Working with Alex was proving to be far more of a challenge than she had envisaged. The truth was, he was still the same charismatic character that she had known when they had been young. He was a born leader, a man to admire and respect, but there was also a warmth about him that drew her in, making her want to get to know him better.

Underneath it all, she still remembered the boy who had sat next to her on a grassy hillside all those years ago, and put his arm around her to comfort her when she had been feeling low. He had been the one who had managed to coax a smile from her and bring the sun into her life when all had been rain. She had loved him then with an adolescent fervour, but they had parted and gone their separate ways, and now that she had found him again she was wary of letting her heart rule her head. He was popular with everyone and she was in too vulnerable a state to risk being hurt.

Nathan leaned back in his chair. 'You're bound to be cautious about working in A and E after what happened. Lives are at stake and it puts a tremendous burden of responsibility on your shoulders. You shouldn't flog yourself. From what you've told me, and as hard as you were on yourself, you didn't do anything wrong.'

Sunlight poured in through the kitchen window and highlighted his brown hair, burnishing it with patches of gold. He was around the same age as Alex, but his was a more serious personality, and he was generally more given to deep thinking and measured responses. It went along with his job as a lawyer, Katie supposed, but he had a sense of humour and she liked him. He had been helpful and friendly towards her from the first, and she was glad to have him living nearby.

'I can't see that there will be any problem arising out of the misadventure in surgery,' he went on. 'After all, your former consultant isn't making an issue out of it. Some surgical situations are trickier than others and things will go wrong from time to time. The only worry would be if the patient himself decided to make a case for compensation, because of prolonged illness due to surgical error or something like that. He would have to prove his case, of course, and he would need to bring the action within a certain time limit. You would be notified of what was happening.'

Katie bit her lip. 'I suppose there's a possibility he

might do that. The man's relatives were unhappy about his prolonged stay in hospital.'

Nathan made a face. 'If I were in your position, I wouldn't worry about it until I heard otherwise.' He sipped at his tea and helped himself to another slice of toast, spreading it with a thin film of orange marmalade. 'Anyway, if you do have any problems from that quarter, I could ask around among my colleagues and find someone who specialises in those types of cases—unless, of course, the hospital's lawyers take it over.'

'Thank you.' It was good to know that he was on her side, but Katie was still uneasy. What if Alex was to discover that there was a potential lawsuit hanging over her? Ought she to warn him about the possibility? Then again, the question hadn't come up, and might never be a problem. Why should she muddy the waters unnecessarily?

'What about you, Jessica?' Nathan asked, between mouthfuls of toast. 'How are you getting on? Are you staying on here for a while, or will you be going back home?'

Jessica finished off her cereal and looked up at him. 'I'm staying,' she murmured. 'Katie says that I can, and Mum's having problems back at the house, so she's happy enough for me to be here.'

'Jess's beginning to make friends in the area,' Katie put in. 'She's put her name down for a lot of the organised activities that are going on through the summer holidays and I think that's helping her to adjust.'

'That's good.' Nathan glanced at Katie. 'It must be

a bit of a worry for you, with Jessica being at home and you going out to work. I know that Sue from down the lane said she would help out if need be, but if you have any problems I'll be working from home on some case notes in the afternoons over the next few weeks, so I'll be around in case of an emergency.'

Katie gave him a smile. 'That's good to know. Thanks.' She glanced at Jessica. 'It helps to have someone close at hand, doesn't it?'

Jessica nodded. 'I like going round to Nathan's house. He has a beautiful fishpond, and it's so peaceful out in his garden.'

Katie laughed. 'If you like gardens so much, you could set to with a rake, a spade and a hoe in ours. It's a jungle out there.'

It was some half an hour later, after Katie had cleared away the breakfast dishes and seen Jessica off to the activities centre, that she started out for the hospital.

Alex was already on duty when she arrived in A and E, but there must have been a temporary lull in the intake of casualties because he was chatting to the nurses and a couple of doctors who were dealing with forms and writing up charts at the central desk. There was a lot of laughter and Sarah, especially, was standing close to him, her hand resting on his arm in an intimate gesture.

'If you want to make this place the best,' she was saying with a chuckle, 'you'll have to lift it up en masse and transport it to the new wing. With the best will in the world, there's only so much we can do here. We're nurses, not miracle-workers.'

'Not true,' Alex admonished with a wagging finger. 'I've seen you work wonders day after day. What's the occasional miracle between friends? As to moving to the new wing, just as long as I get to be head of the new unit, everything will be plain sailing. I'll take you all with me and there won't be any such things as waiting times and targets to be met. It'll all work like a dream. You'll see.'

'Yeah, sure.' There was more laughter and the group broke up as a siren sounded in the distance.

'Ah, there you are, Katie,' Alex said coming to meet her. 'You're here sooner than I expected. I wasn't sure how you would cope with these early starts, especially with having Jessica around, but you seem to be managing very well.'

Katie nodded. 'I've always been a lark rather than an owl. Besides, my neighbour is always up and about early and we often have breakfast together. He's a lawyer and on several days a week he has to appear in court for his clients early in the morning, so he likes to get up in good time to prepare for the day.'

'It sounds like an ideal situation.' Alex sent her an odd look. 'I take it he has no family of his own?'

'No, he doesn't. He's fairly new to the area, like me. He's around your age, and he's not a natural loner. I think he quite likes the company.'

Alex's blue-grey eyes held a sober expression. 'Yes, I expect he does.' He picked up a chart from the desk and handed it to her. 'I'd like you to take a look at the patient in treatment room four, if you will. She's a woman in her late fifties, complaining of fever and chills, and chest pain that's radiating into the middle of her back. Colin took a look at her earlier, and noted that there's some stiffness in her neck. He's querying whether it's meningitis, so he did a lumbar puncture and ordered blood and urine tests, but he had to leave to attend a meeting. Perhaps you would take over in his absence?'

'Of course.' She was a little bemused by his change in manner. Just a moment ago, when he had been talking with Sarah, he had been all smiles, but now that camaraderie had vanished and he was totally professional once more. Perhaps he and Sarah were especially close? A small tremor ran through her limbs. Why did that thought bother her?

She pushed it out of her mind and went along to see her patient. 'Mrs Clark, hello,' she said. 'I'm Dr Sorenson and I've been asked to examine you while Dr Davies is busy elsewhere. I understand you've been having some chest pain?'

'I've a headache, too.' The woman frowned. Her hair was black but sprinkled heavily with strands of silver and her complexion was generally pale, except for bright spots of colour in her cheeks. 'Do you know what's wrong with me?'

Katie glanced at the lab results. 'It looks as though you have a urinary tract infection, and Dr Davies thinks you may have meningitis—an inflammation of the protective membranes that cover the nervous system. The results of the lumbar puncture seem to point to that, and it would certainly account for the headache and the stiffness in your neck.'

The woman looked worried. 'Is it serious?'

'It could have been, but now that we have a diagnosis we can begin treatment right away. I think the best course of action would be to start you off on some antibiotics. I'll ask the nurse to come and see you and make you a little more comfortable, and I'll pop by to see you in a little while.'

'Thanks, dear.' She winced with pain as she tried to adjust her position slightly in the bed. 'My husband will be pleased that you found out what's wrong, anyway. He worries, you know.'

Katie gave her a smile and left the room, going in search of a nurse. She worked her way through her list of patients, and it was a couple of hours later when she next popped in to see Mrs Clark.

'How are you doing?' she asked.

'I'm not sure,' the woman answered. 'I have this horrible pain in my chest and I feel a bit strange. It's probably lying in bed for such a long while that's doing it. I'm used to being up and about.'

'She says her legs are a bit tingly,' her husband put in. 'I expect it's because she's had to stay in one position for so long.'

'That could be it,' Katie agreed. 'I'll ask one of the nurses to come along and give her a leg massage to see if that will improve the circulation.' Katie left the room once more and made up her mind to mention the tingling to Dr Davies. She went in search of him. Perhaps he was back from his meeting by now.

Colin was in his office, she discovered, but he didn't think there was any significance in Mrs Clark's latest symptom when she mentioned it to him.

'She's perhaps still a bit sore from the lumbar puncture,' he said, 'and we need to give the antibiotics time to work.'

'Yes, you're probably right,' she murmured doubtfully. 'I just have a feeling that we ought to be doing more checks, just in case.'

'I wouldn't have thought that was necessary,' he said. 'We've already diagnosed the meningitis.'

'Yes.' She glanced at him. 'Are you back to work on her case now?'

'Not yet. I need to sort out these notes from my meeting and I have to go out again in a while. I'll leave her with you for the next hour or so, if you don't mind.'

'OK.'

She left him and went back to the desk so that she could glance through her lab test results.

'Is anything wrong?' Alex caught up with her as she was crossing the main thoroughfare of A and E just a short time later.

She shook her head, sending the bright mass of her chestnut curls quivering in response. 'No, nothing at all. I was just mulling something over in my head.'

'From your frown, it looks as though it must be a weighty problem. You haven't had a break since you started work this morning, have you? Perhaps you should come along with me to the doctors' lounge and get a cup of coffee.'

She nodded agreement. 'That sounds like a good idea.'

They walked into the doctors' lounge together, and Alex poured coffee while she idly scanned the notice-board.

'It says here that the new wing is due to be opened in the autumn,' she noted. 'Isn't that what you were all talking about this morning? Is there any chance that A and E will be moved over to there?'

'That's what we're all hoping for. It was purpose built, but there's some question now as to whether we'll stay here and take care of a certain category of injuries, while another team will take over that department. It would be a promotion for me if I were to be given the job of heading the unit. It all depends how things go here, I suppose. I've a good team behind me, but it's how management views the situation that matters in the end.'

'I can see why you would want to move there. Judging by these sketches, it's going to be a fabulous place.' She studied him for a moment or two. 'I imagine management is very taken with you. From what I've heard, you have a great record for making changes that improve the way the department operates. That must count for a lot, surely?'

'Let's hope so. I like it when things run smoothly. So far everything is going well. I just need to keep it that way.'

Katie nodded, but his comment disturbed her. She

was beginning to settle to the work in this emergency department, but how would it be if her troubles from her former hospital came to haunt her here? How safe would her job be then?

'You look as though there's something on your mind. Is everything working out all right with Jessica? What are the chances of her going home?'

'None just now. My mother is having a hard time of it. Jessica's father seems to be irritable a lot of the time and things aren't going too well. Mum rang the other day to talk to us, and I had the impression that she wants to leave things as they are for a while. Knowing my mother and my stepfather, I guess that means for a long time to come. Jessica's happy enough with that arrangement, anyway.'

'But what about your feelings? What happens if you decide that you want to be with someone—maybe you'll meet up with the love of your life and want to set up home with him? Isn't Jessica going to be in the way?'

Katie gave him a wry smile. 'That isn't going to happen. I've seen too many couples that think they've fallen in love, only to see their relationships disintegrate. I've watched it for myself firsthand, and it isn't something I want to go through for myself. I think I prefer to keep things light-hearted.'

He gave her a guarded look. 'You may change your mind about that.'

Katie might have answered him, but her phone rang just then, and she flipped it open to take the call.

It was the project leader from the activity centre. 'I'm ringing to ask you why Jessica hasn't turned up,' the woman said. 'We were expecting her to be here for 9 o'clock this morning, but so far there's been no sign of her. Is she ill? If so, we would appreciate it if you would let us know before registration.'

'I don't understand,' Katie said. 'I saw her to the bus stop this morning. Are you sure that she isn't somewhere else in the building or in the grounds?'

'I'm quite positive. I wouldn't be ringing you if I hadn't checked first.'

'I'm sorry. I'll have to look into this. Thank you for ringing me and letting me know.' Katie cut the call and stared down at the phone in her hand as though it was about to explode.

Alex was indented. 'I take it that Jessica isn't where she's supposed to be? That sounds somehow familiar.'

Katie stared at him. 'She hasn't run away. I left her at the bus stop this morning with her friend and she was looking forward to the day ahead. There's no reason for her to take off.'

'Does she have her phone with her? Can't you give her a ring?'

Katie nodded. 'Yes, of course…I'll do that.'

Sarah put her head round the door of the doctors' lounge just then. 'Alex, we've a road traffic accident injury coming in. Broken bones and suspected internal injuries. ETA five minutes.'

'I'll be there.'

Sarah left as Katie was dialling the number. 'She's

not answering.' She began to pace the room. 'Where on earth can she be?'

'If she's with her friend, I doubt she'll get into too much bother. Perhaps you should try her number again in a few minutes.'

'Yes, I will.' She stared around her anxiously, her mind flitting in all directions. 'I should go and check on Mrs Clark. She wasn't feeling too well. I know that she has meningitis, but I'm not sure that the antibiotics are the whole answer.'

Alex's brow furrowed. 'What did you have in mind?'

She looked up at him, her gaze cloudy. 'I don't know. I can't think straight. Perhaps I should just admit her to a medical ward. That would be the next logical step. It's just that one or two of the symptoms don't add up and I feel that I'm missing something.'

She started to key in a text message on the phone. 'Jessica wouldn't run away. I know she wouldn't. She only did it in the first place because she wanted to get away from an untenable situation.'

'Maybe she simply went back to your house for some reason. If that's so, perhaps your neighbour will have seen her.'

Katie let out a shaky breath. 'That's true. I'll ring home and then give Nathan a call. I should try Sue's number as well.'

A couple of minutes later she was still no wiser. Neither of her neighbours had seen Jessica and her friend, and when she tried the cottage, the phone rang in an empty house.

'Would you like me to ask Martin to take over your patients for you?' Alex was clearly concerned. 'You're obviously distracted and in no fit state to go on working.'

He came over to her and placed his hands on her arms, circling her smooth flesh with his palms. It was a gentle, caressing gesture, and Katie looked up at him, her gaze bewildered.

'I don't know. I suppose he could arrange for Mrs Clark to be transferred.'

'If you think that's what needs to be done. I'll see to it for you.' His voice was gentle, soothing, as though he was pacifying a child.

She blinked. She was supposed to be an experienced A and E doctor. It wasn't right that she should collapse under pressure, but everything was going wrong and she couldn't concentrate while he was holding her this way.

'I… No, don't involve Martin. I'll be all right. I just need to get myself together. Jessica can't be in any danger, can she? She wasn't on her own. She has her phone with her. If there was a problem, she would get in touch with me, wouldn't she?'

'Yes, I would think so.' He released her and took a step backwards. 'Though, if she missed the bus, she might not want to worry you unnecessarily. Perhaps she didn't realise that the head of the centre would ring you when she didn't turn up. And if she's with her friend, they might simply have decided to go and do their own thing. That's what teenagers are all about, isn't it? They don't see the need for rules and regulations and being in the right place at the right time.'

'Jessica isn't like that.' She glared at him. 'She's my sister, and I trust her. I don't know why you have to look on the negative side where she's concerned.'

'Maybe it's because this isn't the first time she's taken matters into her own hands. Perhaps you don't know your sister as well as you think you do.'

Katie braced her shoulders. 'I've sent her a text message. Perhaps she'll get back to me in a while.' She hesitated, staring around the room before pulling in a deep breath and heading towards the door. 'I'll go and check on Mrs Clark.'

He went with her, and she wondered if he didn't trust her to do her job properly. 'What are you planning to do? Do you think you've looked properly at all the options? Are you going to go ahead and transfer her?'

She shook her head. 'No, that can come later. I think I need to do an MRI. I know it may not be strictly necessary, but something is bothering me, and I want to be on the safe side.'

'So you're going to do an MRI based purely on instinct?'

'Are you telling me that I shouldn't? I know I should justify it, but it's simply that I feel that there's something I'm not seeing. I know she's Colin's patient, but he left me in charge. It's my decision and I'm prepared to stand by it.'

'By all means go ahead and do the MRI. I wouldn't deny that instinct is a powerful force. I use it myself quite frequently.' He smiled briefly. 'Let me know the result.'

'I will.'

She hurried away to set the wheels in motion. The fact that Jessica hadn't answered her text message was playing on her mind the whole time. What was going on? Was she in any danger? Perhaps she ought to hand over her patients to Martin and go out and look for her. But where would she start?

And why was Alex so sure that her sister was simply playing truant? Did he not care that she might be in trouble? What kind of man was he?

# CHAPTER SIX

'I DON'T know how I'm going to be able to work with these changes in shift patterns, Alex.' Sarah was distraught as she wafted a paper in front of him. 'In fact, all of the nurses are up in arms about them. Just look at these schedules.'

Katie watched as the girl ran a hand through her fair hair. Thankfully, her own problems had faded into the distance a little. It had been half an hour since she had taken the call from the woman in charge of the activity centre, and Jessica had at least replied to Katie's text message, so that she knew she was safe.

Alex ran his gaze over the papers. 'They do seem a little ambitious,' he commented.

'Impossible is the word,' Sarah said with heavy emphasis. 'I've tried talking to the nursing manager about it, but she says it's out of her hands. She told me that the administration chiefs are determined to bring in new contracts and if we don't sign we could all be out of a job.'

'That isn't going to happen,' Alex said. 'Think about it. How could they possibly maintain the A and E unit without the nurses? We'd grind to a halt in no time at all.'

Sarah was still distressed. 'But she said they were planning on bringing in agency staff to fill any gaps. She's tried talking to them, but they're not listening. I'm worried, Alex. I love working here, but I don't like all these changes that they're proposing. They'll be too disruptive.'

Alex put an arm around the young woman and drew her close. 'I'll go and have a word with management. I'm sure it's just some harebrained idea that they've thought up to smooth things over when the new unit is up and running. I'll persuade them that it won't work. Don't worry about it. I'm sure I can make them stop and see sense.'

Sarah looked up at him, her mouth relaxing a fraction. 'Thanks, Alex. You're a treasure. I don't know where I'd be without you.'

He gave her shoulder a little squeeze. 'I'm here for you,' he said softly. 'You know that.'

She nodded, and he released her slowly so that she gathered herself up and moved back to the desk. 'I'm all right. I'll be fine now.'

'That's good.' He gave her a smile and picked up a file from the rack. 'I'd better go and check up on my patients.'

Katie moved to one side as he swivelled around and started off in her direction. He was a busy man, but he always seemed to be able to find the time to help people with their problems. He was never tense or out of sorts and that was one of his strengths. Even so, there was genuine warmth in the way he had spoken to Sarah and held her, and Katie couldn't help wondering if he and the nurse were more than just friends. For some reason, the thought was disturbing, and a tight knot formed in her abdomen.

He glanced at her. 'Is there any news of Jessica?'

'Yes.' She straightened her shoulders. 'She got back to me just a few minutes ago. She said something about missing the bus, but I've told her to make her way here to the hospital. She'll have to wait in the doctors' lounge and amuse herself for a while until I'm off duty.'

'So, she's all right. That must be a relief for you.'

She nodded. 'It is. I was out of my mind with worry for a while.'

He frowned. 'Yes, I could see that you were upset. We should be thankful that it all turned out to be nothing in the end.' He studied her closely for a moment or two. 'Did you get the MRI results back for Mrs Clark?'

Katie sucked in a deep breath at his change of tack. Of course he needed to get back to hospital business as soon as possible. That was how it should be. What else had she expected? He had a department to run, and he couldn't afford to spend any more time on the difficulties that popped up in her private life.

'Yes, I did. I was just going to show them to you. It looks to me as though there's an abscess on her spine. It appears to be quite large, and I think that would account for the chest pain she was experiencing. I imagine the abscess must be pressing on a nerve root.'

'That sounds quite likely. Let's go and take a look at the films.'

'All right.' They walked over to the light box and Katie displayed the films for him to see. 'It's there, around the T4-T5 level,' Katie observed. 'If it gets any larger, I'm afraid that it will threaten the spinal cord and she will start to suffer some degree of paralysis or at the very least weakness in her legs. That process already seems to be under way.'

'I agree with you.' Alex's expression was grim as he studied the films. 'It doesn't bear thinking about what might have happened if you had sent her up to the medical ward. They might have simply accepted the diagnosis of meningitis and by the time they eventually realised otherwise, the damage would have been done and this problem would have been irreversible. Antibiotic cover alone isn't a particularly satisfactory way of managing situations like these.'

He turned to give her a sideways look. 'It just goes to show that you can't allow yourself to be distracted when you're on duty.' His mouth firmed. 'Having your sister around is a responsibility that you could do without. She's getting in the way of your ability to do your job.'

Katie was taken aback by his blunt warning. 'But I didn't transfer the patient in the end, did I? Aren't you judging me a little too harshly—in the same way that you condemn Jessica, too?'

'Am I? You were debating whether to send the woman

off to another department. Can't you admit that you came within a hair's breadth of doing that? The lesson is that you need to look at all the differentials when you're dealing with patients, and if your mind is clouded by troubles at home then you might miss something and it could be that the patients are the ones who suffer.'

'Wouldn't you have agreed to the transfer? I thought we even had a discussion as to whether the MRI was necessary?'

'That's true, we did, but I wanted to see what you would do. My position here means that I have to oversee what goes on and actually, no, I wouldn't have agreed to the transfer. I would have carried out other checks first.'

Katie was in shock. So he had been testing her, and she had been found wanting. It was true that she had been anxious when she had learned that Jessica was not at the activity centre, but she had pulled herself together in time, hadn't she? Why was he being so hard on her? Did she deserve all this disapproval?

Her confidence was shot to pieces all over again, but she had no choice but to push her emotions to one side. Her patient's well-being was at stake and she had to concentrate on that.

'I'll go and arrange for a neurosurgical consultation,' she managed. The abscess would need to be drained so that the pressure on the woman's spine could be alleviated.

He nodded. 'The sooner the better.'

Katie hurried away to make the call. It was becoming

clear that Mrs Clark would have to be prepped for surgery and she hoped that the woman hadn't had anything to eat or drink in the last few hours. Any delay could be dangerous.

A short time later she called on Sarah to assist in getting her patient ready. 'She's going up to operating theatre number two,' she told the nurse. 'Will you stay with her? Things have taken a different turn quite suddenly and there may be a lot of questions she still needs to ask.'

'I will.' Sarah sent Katie a quick look. 'I couldn't help hearing some of what Alex was saying to you. I came back to get some papers—I must say I think he was a bit hard on you. You did the right thing in keeping her here and doing an MRI. I'm not so sure that any of the other doctors who took over the case would have picked up on the diagnosis. They would probably have just accepted meningitis and gone with that. Anyway, she's Colin's patient, isn't she? He's the one who would bear the ultimate responsibility.'

'But the patient is the one who might have spent her life being paralysed,' Katie said in a low voice. 'I have to live with that and I can't help thinking that Alex was right to point it out.'

'Don't let it get you down.' Sarah's gaze was sympathetic. 'Alex isn't usually so harsh. It might be that he's concerned about the new unit. It's due to open soon and they still haven't made the decision about who's going to run it. He has to work out how he's going to handle things if he does get the job—and live with the aftermath if he doesn't.'

'I know. Thanks.' It was good of Sarah to take the time and trouble to try to comfort her, but Katie was desolate. How many more mistakes were going to be laid at her door? She should never have come back into medicine.

Jessica arrived at the unit a few minutes later. She appeared timid as she crept quietly through the double doors, as though she hoped she wouldn't be seen. Katie was glancing through a chart that Alex had handed to her, but she looked up as the girl tried to blend in with one of the curtains that separated the main thoroughfare from the annexe.

'There you are,' Katie said, frowning. 'I've been so worried about you. What happened? How did you come to miss the bus this morning?'

'We—Sophie and I thought we had time to go over to the shop,' Jessica mumbled. 'We were going to buy some sweets, but there was a queue and it took longer than we thought. I didn't ring you because you were at work and I thought you might worry if you knew that I wasn't at the centre.' She looked downcast. 'I'm sorry, Katie, really I am.'

'Couldn't you have waited for the next bus to come along?'

Jessica shook her head. 'We wouldn't have been there in time for the start of the day's events. We were supposed to be going on a nature trail, and once we missed that we would have been on our own at the centre.'

Katie could see the logic in her argument. 'Stay at the bus stop next time, instead of wandering off to the shop,' she said, 'and if anything happens and you don't get to where you're supposed to be, give me a call.' Seeing the girl's unhappy expression, she relented and gave her a hug. 'I won't be angry. I just need to know.'

'All right, I will, I promise.'

'Good. Where is your friend, Sophie?'

'She went home.'

'I suppose that's something at least, and I have you back here safe and sound.' Katie glanced at the watch on her wrist. 'There's still some time left before the end of my shift. Have you had anything to eat?'

Jessica shook her head. 'No—well, except for a burger earlier on. I'm starving. When we realised we'd miss the bus, we walked around town for a while, and then we went to a burger stand and sat in the town square to eat.'

'Go along to the hospital café and get yourself something,' Katie said. 'Then come back here and I'll show you into the doctors' lounge. You can sit in there for a while and wait for me.'

Jessica smiled. 'Thanks, Katie. I didn't mean to cause any trouble, honestly.' She made a face. 'If this had happened with Dad around, he'd have gone mad. His temper's awesome. I'm so glad you're not like him.'

Katie's lips flattened. 'Just don't test me to the limit,' she said, 'or you might find that my nerves can be on edge, too. Now, I have to get on, so off you go to the café.'

Jessica didn't need a second bidding. She shot off in the direction of the restaurant and Katie went to find her patient.

She discovered that Alex was waiting for her by the treatment-room door, and she approached him cautiously. What now? Was she in more trouble?

He said quietly, 'I saw that Jessica arrived. Is everything all right with her?'

Katie nodded. 'It was nothing out of the ordinary. She and her friend missed the bus because they were messing about and then they were afraid to let anyone know what had happened.'

'Worry over, then. That's good.' He waved a hand towards the treatment room. 'Would you mind if I come in with you while you take a look at this patient? She's a young woman who has already been seen by one of the medical students. He did a physical examination and because her heart rate is faster than it should be he wants to check her out for heart problems. She's been complaining of dull back pain, nausea, neck pain and headache.'

A second patient with back pain? Katie glanced at him warily. 'Is this another test?'

He shook his head and gave a wry smile. 'No, you can relax. I just want your opinion.'

Was he joking? Somehow she didn't feel in the least able to relax around him. She was churned up inside, filled with conflicting emotions as far as he was concerned. What was she to make of him? He was a strange mix, a vital, energetic version of the boy she had known all those years ago and an authoritative, powerful consultant in charge of a lively, growing emergency unit. She wasn't at all sure how to react to him now that he was her boss.

'All right, then. Shall we go in?' She found it hard to accept that he had no ulterior motive, but she could hardly refuse his request, could she? Katie pushed open the door and he followed her into the room.

'Hello, Jenny,' she greeted the patient. The girl was in her early twenties and dark-haired. She looked distinctly unwell. 'I hear that you've been feeling poorly for quite some time.'

'Yes, I have, but it's my back that's bothering me.' Jenny flopped back against her pillows in agitation. 'The pain is much worse today. It's really getting me down. I feel worn out.' The young woman looked flushed and uncomfortable.

'That's understandable,' Katie murmured. 'Your heart rate is very fast and prolonged episodes of pain can certainly make you feel wretched.' She glanced down at her notes. 'It says here that you had thyroid surgery a few months ago.'

'Yes, I did.' The woman moved restlessly. 'The other doctor said that everything had healed up well.' She looked up at Katie. 'Do you know what's wrong with me?'

'I'm working on it,' Katie said with a smile. She glanced at Alex. 'Are the blood-test results back from the lab?'

'Not yet.'

'I'll give them a ring,' Katie said. 'They might have them now.'

She went to the side of the room to make the call. As she waited for the lab technician to find the paperwork, she saw that Alex had drawn up a chair alongside the bed and was chatting to the girl in a friendly fashion. He managed to make her smile, and Katie wondered at his ability to charm everyone around him.

A minute or two later Katie went to join him at the bedside. 'Your blood tests show a low level of calcium,' she told Jenny. 'I think what's happened is that since your thyroid surgery the levels of parathyroid hormone in your body have fallen, and in turn your blood calcium level is lower than it should be. That's why you're having so many uncomfortable symptoms. We should be able to sort that out for you quite easily by prescribing you some tablets.'

Jenny's face lit up. 'You can? That's wonderful.'

Katie was pleased that she had managed to get to the bottom of the problem. When she left the room with Alex a few minutes later, he said, 'I thought you handled that very well. It was good that you took the initiative and phoned for the results instead of keeping her in suspense.'

'Does that mean that I've managed to redeem myself?' Her expression was bemused. 'After what happened this morning, I wondered if I might be on my way to looking for another job in the near future.'

'That is very unlikely, isn't it?' He gave her a quizzical look. 'You signed a contract, didn't you?'

'But it only lasts for a few months. When it comes to an end, I'm going to be faced with the dilemma of whether or not I'll be kept on.' She studied him from under her lashes. 'Isn't that why you were watching me…to see if I make any mistakes?'

'That's not the case at all.' He walked with her over to the central desk.

'Isn't it?' She wasn't convinced. 'Weren't you keeping an eye on me earlier to see if I was about to mess things up?'

His glance flitted over her. 'You really need to have more faith in yourself and your abilities. I think you might have misunderstood my intentions. I wasn't putting you on trial earlier, or trying to catch you out in any way. I wanted you to work things out for yourself. Afterwards, I was pointing out that if you come to a situation where something bothers you, and threatens to get in the way of you doing your job properly, you need to be able to admit to it and hand over to someone else. No one will think any less of you, but you can't give your best to patients when you're under stress.'

'Oh, I see.' She blinked. 'At least, I think I do…'

He laid a hand on her shoulder. 'Katie, you have to understand that for the most part I trust your judgement, and it occurred to me that if things work out well, you might be considered as someone who could mentor individual medical students. We're always looking for good, skilled doctors who can provide extra support for others throughout their training.'

Her brows lifted in astonishment. 'I had no idea. I thought I was in big trouble.'

His palm slid down over her bare arm in a silken caress. 'It's time that you start to believe in yourself. I don't know what happened to make you feel this way, but you can't simply crumble at every hint of criticism. Can't you tell me what went wrong to make you so anxious about doing your job?'

Katie pulled in a quick breath. Her mind was racing. Should she tell him what had happened at her former hospital? How would he look on her if she did that? Would he ignore her side of the story and simply condemn her? She couldn't bear it if he did that.

'Working in A and E is such a huge responsibility,' she said huskily. 'All day long we're making life and death decisions. I think the strain was too much for me.'

'You're not on your own, Katie. You should remember that. There's always going to be someone who will support you and help you to work through any worries you have. As for me, I'm your supervisor, but I hope I'm a lot more to you than that...we can't simply ignore the friendship we had in the past, can we?' His grey-blue glance meshed with hers. 'We shared the bad times together and came through them unscathed, so surely we can face up to the future without falling apart?'

'I suppose so.' His hand on her arm was warm and supportive, drawing her near to him so that she was breathtakingly conscious of his long body next to hers. He was strong and supple, full of vibrant energy, and more than anything she wanted to stay by his side, caught up in his warm embrace.

'I think you need cheering up,' he murmured, his gaze drifting over her. 'You'll be off duty tomorrow, won't you? We could take a boat trip out on Lake Windermere, if you like. The weather's been beautiful these last few days and it's forecast to go on being sunny and warm, so we could take advantage of it. I'm sure it would do you good to leave this place behind you for a while.'

She drew in a quick breath, startled by his spontaneous invitation. It was a tempting thought—that she might seize the chance to spend a few hours with him, enjoying the fresh air and sunshine without a care in the world.

'That's a lovely idea,' she said softly, 'only I don't think I can go along with it. I have Jessica living with me now. I have to fit my life around her.'

'Won't she be going off on one of her organised days out?'

'No. We only arrange those for when I'm at work. The rest of the time we like to spend together. I want to make up to her for the times when she felt alone.'

He was thoughtful for a second or two. 'Well, it's no problem. We'll all go. We could go on board one of the steamboats and take a leisurely trip along the length of the lake. We could even get something to eat and drink while we're on board.' He looked at her, his eyes wide and dancing with light. 'What do you think?'

When he gazed at her that way, she felt her insides go into meltdown, and she smiled up at him. 'I'd like that. I'm sure Jessica will, too.'

He looked pleased with himself. 'I'll call for you in the morning, around 11 o'clock, if that's all right with you?'

'That's fine.'

* * *

Alex was as good as his word, and arrived some fifteen minutes early. Jessica was still in the process of getting ready for their day out, but Katie had everything in hand and was in the middle of watering the plants in the garden when she heard his car pull up.

'I'm round the back,' she called to him from the side gate. 'I'll just finish off seeing to these flowers and then I'll be ready to go.' She grinned at him. 'I can't say the same for Jessica—she's been straightening her hair for the last hour.'

He gave her an answering smile as he came into the garden. 'I don't suppose you even think about doing that with yours. You'd be fighting a losing battle from the first, wouldn't you?' His gaze went to the mass of tawny curls that rioted around her temples and skimmed the delicate slope of her shoulders. 'You look good,' he said, his mouth tilting as his glance trailed over the smooth outline of her clinging cotton top and moved to caress the gently curving line of her hips. 'I haven't seen you in jeans for years, but I can definitely say that you fill them out well these days.'

Her cheeks filled with faint warmth. He looked spectacular, she thought. He was wearing a casual shirt that matched the colour of his eyes, and was open at the neck to reveal the bronzed column of his throat. His chinos were dark, drawing her attention to the long line of his legs and the leanness of his flat stomach, so that she had to make herself take slow, even breaths to calm the quick tempo of her heartbeat.

It wouldn't do for her to get herself into a tizzy over

him. He was being a good friend, spending time with her for old times' sake, but she shouldn't read anything more into it than that, should she? Neither of them was the same person they had been all those years ago. They had gone their separate ways, and life had changed each of them, so that now heading up a unit was his driving force and a yearning for family stability was hers. The childish part of them that had looked for mutual companionship had gone for ever.

'I'll just finish off here,' she said, 'and with any luck, Jessica will be ready to go.' She emptied the dwindling contents of the watering can over the flower border that she was trying to nurture. 'The garden's a mess, and I really need to tackle it before the weeds take over, but other things keep getting in the way. I told myself I would make a start by planting this section and I'm hoping at least this part will be full of colour by mid summer.'

'I expect it will all come together in the end,' he said, looking around. 'Actually, it's not so bad. You've a lovely rockery in that corner, and a pleasant shrub garden over by the wall. I shouldn't imagine it would take too much work to get it in order.'

'Do you have a place of your own? You said that you lived not too far away from here, didn't you?'

'I have a house a few miles away. It's stone built, the same as this one, but it's more compact, a bit like a stable block with an upper storey. I quite like living there. The house is on a slope, looking out over the fells. It's great in the summer, but not so good in the winter when there's snow about. I have to dig my way out of the drive then,' he said drily. 'The garden's a good size, and I can look out over the fields from there.'

'It sounds lovely,' she said. 'We're both a long way from the children's home, aren't we? I remember you said that you used to live in an old terraced house with your parents, and mine was much the same kind of property. My dad was struggling to make his way in a boat-building business, and there wasn't much money to spare.'

'I don't recall much about my early years,' he said. 'Perhaps I've tried to blot them out.'

She nodded. 'I don't suppose it mattered very much what kind of house we lived in as long as we had family around, but it didn't work out that way for you, did it?'

He shook his head, and Katie looked into his eyes, but his expression was unreadable. She shook the last drops of water over the plants and stared down at them for a moment or two, lost in thought.

'I'll put this away in the shed, and then we'll go into the house and see how Jessica's doing, shall we?'

Thankfully, Jessica was ready at last, so they gathered up bags and jackets and hurried out to Alex's car.

'How long will this boat trip last?' Jessica wanted to know when they were nearly at their destination. 'Do we get to go up on deck?'

'It depends whether we go on the full round trip or whether we stop off somewhere along the way,' Alex answered. 'We can always get back on another boat and continue the journey. You please yourself whether you go up on deck or spend some time in the cabin, whatever you want to do. They have a catering service on board, so we can have drinks and a meal while we watch the scenery go by.'

'That's cool,' Jessica said. 'I vote we go the whole round trip. That way I get to spend a lot of time on deck as well as having something to eat. Do they serve ice-cream desserts? I love ice cream, especially with fresh fruit.'

'I imagine so.' Alex gave her a quick glance in the rear-view mirror. 'It sounds as though you're looking forward to this trip. Have you never been out on the lake before?'

'No, never. Do you think I'll be seasick?' Her mouth turned downwards as she pondered the possibility.

'Let's hope not.' He teased. 'I suppose that will depend on how much ice cream you scoff.'

The boat was already moored by the side of the lake when they arrived at the dock, and they went on board and chose a prime position on the open deck.

'Just look at that view,' Jessica said, scanning the horizon and taking in the sweep of the landscape from Waterhead over the length of Lake Windermere. 'It's awesome.'

Katie went to join her at the boat rail. 'I should have brought my camera,' she murmured. 'You're right, it's beautiful…all those meandering swirls of water, and the wooded hillsides…and the houses tucked away in the valleys.'

'You can use my camera, if you like.' Alex handed

it to her. 'Whatever you take I'll print out for you once we get back home. It's a hobby of mine. I love collecting landscapes. They make me feel peaceful when everything else is chaotic.'

'I can understand that. Thank you.' Katie accepted his offer with a grateful smile as Jessica moved away to go and look out over the water from another vantage point. 'How do I operate it?'

'Like this.' He came to stand behind her, the length of his body against hers, his arms coming around her to set the angle of the camera. 'Look at the display screen or use the viewfinder, whichever you want. Then press this button. See?'

'Yes. I see.' Katie's voice came out as a breathy whisper. She hadn't been expecting the sudden closeness, and the fact that his arms were wrapped around her and his cheek was nestled close to hers made her senses soar in rippling disarray.

She took several shots, thankful that she managed to keep her fingers steady, and then she handed the camera back to him.

'I expect you have pictures from all around the world,' she said. 'You always said that you wanted to travel.'

'Yes. But I've discovered that I actually love this part of England most of all.' He looked over towards the houses that nestled among the trees on the distant shore. 'I think my dream would be to live somewhere like that, in a perfect green setting, with a view that spanned the water and the mountains beyond.'

'Me, too.' She sent him an oblique glance. 'You

talked about the Lake District when we were young. Had you already visited this area?'

'I had an aunt who lived around here when she was first married. She sent us pictures from time to time. My mother talked about her occasionally when she was in one of her better states, but we never came over here for a visit, and I think my aunt went to live abroad after a while, so we lost touch. My mother had thrown the photos into a drawer and forgotten about them, but I rescued them and put them into a folder.'

'Do you see your parents at all? Are they still around?'

'My father died of a drug overdose, and my mother went into rehab.' He grimaced. 'She was always in or out of rehab. I don't think she could face up to life. I don't know what went wrong, but her own family were never there for her and she just seemed to waft about, like driftwood being tossed about on a beach. Having a child to look after was one problem too many, and I think she gave up. I do go and see her quite often, but it doesn't always work out too well. She doesn't seem to have the wherewithal to lift herself out of her cycle of drink and depression.'

'I'm sorry. That must be hard for you.'

'No, it isn't. I knew a long while ago that I wasn't going to be able to rely on my parents. I learned how to cope and I'm happy with the way my life is. I'm stronger for it, and my philosophy is that what you never have you never miss.'

He laid a hand on the deck rail and turned his face towards the oncoming warm breeze, so that it ruffled his hair lightly. 'It was because of my parents that I decided to take up medicine. I thought there had to be a way to help people and prevent them from getting into that state. I'm not sure that it's always possible to do that, but I do what I can, and I found, in the end, that working in emergency medicine is the best place for me. It makes me feel good about myself.'

His gaze drifted over her. 'Strange, isn't it, that you should make the same career move?'

'Perhaps it is. I suppose, deep down, we must be two of a kind.'

He smiled. 'I think maybe we are.' He moved closer to her, his head bending a little so that she could feel the warmth of his skin next to hers. His gaze was concentrated on the softness of her lips, and before she had time to guess his intent he was kissing her, a delicate brush of his mouth on hers, one that sent tremors of sweet sensation coursing through her entire body.

His arm slid around her waist. 'You know,' he said in a roughened voice, 'I've been wanting to do that ever since we met up at the hospital. I don't know quite what came over me, but you looked so lost and distracted when you came away from your interview for the rehab post, and I wanted to gather you up and tell you that it didn't matter.'

'Did you?' She gazed up at him. Try as she may, she couldn't get her mind to function on a normal level. Her head was off in the clouds somewhere, waiting for her nervous system to realign itself, and it wasn't going to do that any time soon, while he was holding her to him.

Then he kissed her again and she was done for, because his lips pressured hers and the foundations of her world began to rock.

'What are you two doing?' Jessica's voice came to her ears and the mist of heat that had wrapped itself around Katie and enveloped her in an enchanted bubble dissolved in a blast of cold air. 'You're not actually kissing, are you?' She scowled. 'And people have the nerve to tell me how to behave… This is a public place, you know.'

Alex cautiously let his arm drop away from her and Katie looked dazedly at her sister. 'I… We… It was just…'

'We were getting to know one another all over again, that's all.' Alex said. 'We used to be friends years ago.'

'Oh, that's a new one, I must say.' Jessica's tone was full of mockery. 'You should watch out for him,' she said, turning back to look at Katie. 'All the nurses have a thing for him, you know. I heard them talking when I was in your restroom at the hospital. It seems to me you have a lot of competition there.'

Alex lifted a brow at that. 'It was just a kiss, Jessica.'

Jessica pulled a face. 'Well, it's a good job nobody but me was looking.'

Katie sent Alex a guarded look. She had to acknowledge that for all her innocence Jessica was probably right about the competition. Hadn't he been cosying up to Sarah only yesterday? She tried to gather herself together.

'It was nothing,' she murmured. 'Like Alex said, we knew each other a long time ago. Put it down to nostalgia.'

'What's that when it's about?' Jessica wrinkled her nose.

'It means it's time for us to go and get you some ice cream,' Alex said. 'Shall we go below deck?'

'Oh, yes,' Jessica said, brightening. 'I'm up for that.'

Katie gave a soft, shuddery sigh. It just went to show that a clear blue sky and a beautiful landscape could cloud her mind with the romance of the moment and banish her inhibitions into the mist. But Alex wasn't the staying kind, was he? From now on she would have to keep a much tighter hold on her emotions where he was concerned.

# CHAPTER SEVEN

'YOU'RE looking very pleased with yourself.' Katie's glance flicked over Alex as she met him in the hospital cafeteria the next day. There was a spring in his step and he exuded energy from every pore.

She scanned the display of desserts and paused to add a fruit salad to her tray, moving her curry and rice to one side to make room for it.

'Yes, I think I am.' He chose a roast dinner with a selection of vegetables and then moved further along the counter to pick out apple pie and cream for afterwards. 'I've just come from a meeting with management, and things went a lot better than I expected.'

Together they moved towards the cash desk to pay for their food, and then he began to look around for somewhere to sit. 'Shall we go outside on to the terrace? It's quiet out there and it'll probably be more pleasant than staying indoors to eat. I yearn for fresh air after I've been cooped up inside for a while.'

Katie could well imagine how he would do that.

On the lake yesterday he had been in his element, standing by the boat's rail gazing over the water and surrounding hills.

'All right.' She followed him outside to a table in a sunny corner of the enclosed paved square. There were tubs of brightly coloured flowers set out at intervals, petunias, pink diaschia and trails of delicate white bacopa. White-painted, trellised screens were positioned here and there to provide protection from any slight breeze, lending a touch of privacy to the diners.

'I sometimes think it would be nice to get away from here and drive down to the coast,' he said. 'I love the smell of the sea breeze and the feel of the wind in my hair. I suppose that's why I like being out on the lake. It gives me a feel of being at one with nature.'

'Me, too. I used to love the trips we would go on to the seaside, especially when Jessica was little. She was like a water nymph whenever we got down to the sea.'

They sat down and began to eat. 'So what was it about your meeting that put a smile on your face?' Katie asked. 'Have they offered you the promotion?'

'No, they won't be making that decision for a week or so yet.' He speared a roast potato and began to cut a section from it. 'I went to tackle them about the changes to the nurses' shift patterns, and they've agreed to let the present schedules stand.'

Katie raised her brows. 'How did you manage that?'

'I pointed out how important it was to keep the goodwill of the nurses. Bringing in agency people would work out well enough in the short term, but it wouldn't be sustainable. A lot of nurses do agency work because the irregular hours suit them and they don't want to work on a permanent basis. Management would be exchanging long-term staff for people who are less likely to stick with the department. That way you might lose some nurses who like a fixed routine, and ultimately the temporary staff might decide to move on. There would have been an awful lot of disruption.'

Katie dipped her fork into her curry. 'Even so, I can't see management being happy to see their plans overturned. Will any of this interfere with your chances of promotion?'

He shook his head. 'No, because I came up with a plan of action for the new unit, ways of making things run smoothly. They seemed to be quite taken with the ideas that I suggested. For one thing, I've worked out a more effective triage system and put forward some strategies for bringing in nursing assistants.'

'That's good. Sarah will be pleased that you managed to sort it out.'

'Yes, I imagine she will.' He scooped up carrots and peas and then sent her a quick glance. 'How about you? Do you feel better for your day off? You looked as though you were enjoying being out on the lake.'

'I do. I had a fantastic time. I'm glad that you persuaded me to go with you.' She smiled at him across the table. 'I'd forgotten how good it can be to relax and enjoy the scenery.' It had been all the more thrilling because he had been standing alongside her, pointing out various landmarks along the way and filling her with a sense of exhilaration. As to that kiss…it had stayed with her for a long, long time afterwards. It was a day she would never forget.

'Me, too. It's been a while since I've taken time out to explore the countryside.' He laid down his knife and fork. 'Do you think Jessica had a good time? It was hard to know what she was thinking. One minute she was fine and the next she appeared to be a little subdued.'

'Yes, I noticed that as well.' Katie frowned. 'She was a bit offhand about some parts of the trip, especially afterwards when we came off the boat and walked through the fields. I thought she would enjoy looking at the watermill and then taking a wander through the woods, but she was definitely quieter than usual. On the whole, though, I'd say she was happy to be out there.'

Katie had loved that leisurely stroll through the woods. With Alex by her side everything had been perfect. Sunlight had dappled the leaves as they had followed the paths through the trees, while Jessica had walked across the fallen logs and scrambled up rocky outcrops. Bluebells grew in profusion over the grassy slopes and in little pockets by the side of the brook or under broken branches, and around the margins of the wood Katie had been thrilled to discover the daisy-like white flowers of stitchwort and clusters of pretty red campion.

Later, they had all walked around the perimeter while Jessica had taken photos of the landscape. Alex had taken Katie's hand in his and they had looked out over sweeping yellow fields of oilseed and wide green meadows. Just being with him had been everything she might have hoped for.

'She likes being able to spend time with you,' Alex murmured. 'You're her big sister after all, and I noticed that when you gave her your undivided attention she was fine.'

'Yes, I suppose that's true. Sometimes I think she feels that I'm all she has. At least she's begun to make friends with people of her own age now that she goes to the activity centre. She has friends back home, but I think a couple of them moved away and that made her feel even more unsettled.'

'So where is she today?'

'She went into town with Sophie and another girl. I gave her money to buy clothes, so I expect she'll be having a wonderful time.'

He frowned. 'Isn't it her parents' job to do that?'

'Perhaps it is. My mother keeps saying she'll send some money for her, but then she forgets. It doesn't matter. She seems to have a lot on her mind right now. My stepfather is stressed because redundancies are in the air at work and he's worried about whether he'll be able to keep his job. They're trying to work things out. Having my sister stay with me is giving Jessica a break from all the tension in the air, and it's probably giving my parents the chance to sort themselves out, too.'

'But you're the one who's having to take the strain. It can't be easy for you. You must have come to the Lake District in order to set up a home for yourself and enjoy your independence, but that's all changed now, hasn't it?'

'I don't see it the way you do. I never intended to walk away from my sister or my parents.' She studied him, trying to understand what made him tick. 'You're not a family person at all, are you? I can't imagine what it would be like to have no family to gather around me. It seems terribly sad to me that you missed out on all that.'

'Not really.' He stopped to take a mouthful of apple pie and added, 'You make it sound as though family is everything and that life without them is the worst thing you could imagine, but families can be trouble. I've seen what happens. People fight among themselves, they can be selfish and pick faults and complain if things don't go their way. Like Jessica, each person has their own idea about how things should be, and it's not always easy to keep everyone happy at the same time. I'm glad I don't have to deal with all that.'

Katie frowned. 'I don't really know what the matter was with Jessica. She isn't usually like that. Perhaps she was still a little bit troubled about what's been going on back home and she might have been wishing that it could all be resolved. I thought she would love the boat trip, and I know she enjoyed it, but she's been in a bit of a strange mood ever since we came home.' Katie took a sip of her ice-cold juice.

'She's probably just confused. Teenagers have a hard time trying to make sense of the world. They only see things from their own point of view, and perhaps

Jessica's problem is that she wanted to have your attention all to herself.'

Katie put her glass down and stared at him. 'I hadn't thought of that. She seems to cope well enough when I'm out at work.' Her brows drew together. 'You're very astute, aren't you?'

'Am I?' He finished off his pie and laid down the spoon, reaching for his coffee cup.

'Oh, yes. You profess not to need people, and you say you're used to standing alone, but if that's true, how is it that you understand others so well? With your background, how did you turn out to be so well balanced?'

He laughed. 'I'm glad if you think that's the way I am. All I can say is that I learned about life the hard way. My parents weren't there for me in the usual sense. They were around physically, but mentally they were in a world of their own a lot of the time. Instead of them looking after me, I was often the one who had to take care of them.'

Her glance moved over him, her mouth making an odd shape. 'That must have been hard for you. It was a huge burden for a young child to bear.'

'I didn't see it that way. I learned to look after myself. It made me stronger, and in the end it was all for the best.' His gaze captured hers. 'I'm thankful that I'm not like you, full of angst and concern. Men don't deal in sentiment, Katie. We just get on with life as it is.'

'Perhaps. I'm not convinced about that.' She sipped

at her fruit juice, looking at him over the rim of her glass. 'Do you see very much of your mother? I know you said that your visits didn't always work out too well, but she's still your mother after all.'

He nodded. 'I go and see her every week to make sure that she's OK. There are times when she seems as though she has things in hand. She was very young when I was born and I think I'm finally beginning to understand what made her the way she is. I'm doing what I can to get her the support that she needs. Up to now, the rehab programmes have only been successful up to a point, but I'm looking for something that will make a more definite change in her life.'

Katie's heart warmed to him. There was a lot more to Alex than met the eye. He denied that he had any softer feelings, but she didn't believe that. His background had led him to grow a tough outer shell, and that was the image he presented to the world. He didn't want anyone to see what he was really like inside because that might be a sign of weakness and that would never do. He wasn't even prepared to drop his guard with her.

'I should get back to work,' he said a few minutes later.

Katie nodded. 'I'll walk with you.'

Back in A and E, she struggled to put thoughts of Alex out of her mind. She had a long list of patients to see, and thinking about Alex would only get in the way and cloud her judgement.

'Would you have time to look at another patient?'

Sarah asked her some time later. Katie had gone over to the central desk and was signing off on her charts, getting ready for the handover at the end of her shift. Alex was doing much the same thing.

'I know it's getting late,' Sarah murmured, 'but there's a woman waiting to be seen in treatment room four. She's been here for quite a while. The registrar was going to take a look at her but he's been called away to another patient.'

'All right,' Katie said. 'I'll go and see her. What seems to be the problem?'

'She has a bad headache. She seems to be very anxious and is complaining about tenderness in her scalp. Her GP treated her for tension headache earlier, but her husband brought her in to get a second opinion.'

Sarah turned to Alex. 'And there's a patient in the room next door with a wound to his face. Would you have time to take a look at him before you go off duty? I know it's a bit late to ask, but we're building up quite a backlog and I think he needs to be seen now.'

Alex nodded. 'OK. We were busy dealing with the patients from the traffic accident earlier, so it's unfortunate that other people have had to wait. Just explain to them that we'll get round to everyone as soon as possible. The next shift should be able to handle the majority without too much trouble.'

He put his charts to one side and began to head in the direction of the treatment room. Katie took the patient's notes that Sarah handed to her and began to study them as she walked alongside him.

Monica Jenkins, she discovered, was a slender woman in her mid-forties, who appeared to be quite agitated. 'I can't get rid of this pain in my head,' she said. 'It woke me up this morning and it just won't go away. I don't know what to do. This has well and truly stopped me in my tracks. I've a thousand and one jobs to be getting on with, and I have the family coming round this weekend for a celebration meal.'

'Do you?' Katie smiled at her. 'What's the occasion?'

'A special wedding anniversary. Some people are coming from miles away, and I'm supposed to be getting rooms ready for them. I can't afford to have a headache.'

'I can see how all the tension would get to you,' Katie said. 'Have you ever suffered from migraines?'

'No. I get the odd headache from time to time, but nothing like this. This is awful and the pain is practically unbearable.'

Katie began to examine her, checking for signs of neurological change. 'Have you been feeling sick at all?'

'I was sick just half an hour ago.'

'And is there any neck pain, any problems with your eyes?'

'It hurts if I move my head. It feels as though it's being held in a clamp.' Monica slumped back against her pillows. 'I'm so tired. Could you just give me something for the pain? I took some tablets a few hours ago, but they didn't do any good.'

'Yes, I'll see to that. I'm going to arrange for you to

have a CT scan so that we can find out what's going on. I'll ask the nurse to come and make you more comfortable and then I'll take you down to Radiology.'

Katie left the room and found Sarah waiting for her. 'There's a phone call for you,' she said. 'It's Jessica—she sounds a bit upset.'

'OK, thanks.' Katie frowned. What now? Was Jessica in trouble again?

Alex had finished seeing his patient and was heading towards the desk. He placed the chart in a tray and said to Sarah, 'Mr Gray in room three needs to have his wound cleaned and sutured by a specialist surgeon. Would you ask Mr Grainger to come and look at him, please?'

Sarah nodded. 'I'll get on to it.'

'And as soon as you've done that,' Katie said hurriedly, 'would you take Mrs Jenkins down to Radiology for a CT scan? I was going to go with her, but I need to deal with this first. I'd rather there wasn't any delay in sending her down there.'

'Yes, I'll do that.' Sarah looked surprised. 'You don't think it's a tension headache or a migraine, then? Last time I checked her she wasn't showing any signs other than a raised blood pressure. Even the registrar thought she was going through the beginnings of a migraine.'

Katie nodded. 'I know that, but I can't be sure of anything until I have the results of the scan. I know she doesn't have any focal neurological signs at the moment, but she says the headache woke her up and it seems to be particularly painful. I'd sooner err on the side of caution.'

She looked at Alex and saw that he was frowning. Did he doubt that she was making the right decision, too?

He glanced at Katie as she went over to the phone. 'Do you need me to take over from you?' he asked.

'No, I'm on top of it.' She didn't want him thinking that she couldn't cope or that she would go to pieces every time Jessica called.

She picked up the receiver. 'Hello, is that you, Jessica?'

'Oh, Katie…you have to come and help me. They have me shut up in this room and they won't let me go. They keep asking me questions. I didn't know what to do. I tried to ring Nathan to see if he could help, but he wasn't answering his phone.'

'What do you mean, you're shut up in a room?' Katie felt the blood drain from her face. A shiver ran along her spine. 'Where are you?'

'I'm at the new superstore in town. You know, the one by the bridge. They're saying I took something, but I didn't. I don't know how it got into my jacket pocket. I didn't put it there.' Jessica began to cry. 'You have to come and help me, Katie, please. They're being horrible to me.'

'Who are they?'

'The store people. There's this woman who keeps being nasty to me.'

'Is she there now—can I speak to her?'

'No, there's just me and Sophie and Jade. She went out to fetch someone and there's a man standing guard outside the door.' Jessica made a sobbing sound. 'They won't let us out of the room. The woman said we have to stay here until we admit to stealing.'

'All right, I'll come over to you as soon as I can. Try to calm yourself down. I have to see to my patient before I can leave here, but I won't be too long, I promise.'

Katie was thoroughly shaken by this news. Why would anyone accuse Jessica of stealing? It wasn't like her to do anything like that. But then again, she hadn't turned up at the activities centre the other day when she was supposed to. What was going on with her?

Jessica made a small hiccuping sound. 'What shall I do, Katie?'

'Nothing, for the moment. Don't say anything to anyone at the store and be quiet and sensible with your friends. I'll get over to you as soon as I can.'

She put down the receiver and tried to recover herself. All this had come as a shock, but she had to get herself together and concentrate on what was most important.

She turned to Alex, who was still standing by her side. Sarah was nowhere to be seen. 'Has Sarah taken my patient to Radiology?'

'Yes, she left straight away.' He sent her an assessing glance. 'Are you all right? You look very pale.'

'I'm fine. I just have to sort something out with Jessica as soon as I leave here.'

'Yes, I gather that. I heard some of what you were saying. Is she in trouble again?'

Katie nodded. 'I don't know all the details, but I

think she's been accused of stealing something from one of the stores. I can't understand it. Jessica doesn't do that kind of thing.'

He made a face. 'It's beginning to sound as though Jessica does lots of things that you don't expect of her. This must be the third time that she's called you to get her out of some scrape or another. I can almost see why your parents were beginning to lose patience with her.'

Katie sent him a sharp look. 'You're just assuming that she's in the wrong. We don't know that. She's going through a difficult time, and she needs my support. I'm not going to let her down when she's relying on me.'

'I wasn't suggesting that you should. I was just pointing out that this is getting to be a regular occurrence.'

'And you think it's getting in the way of my work?' She gave a sigh of frustration. 'Whatever is going on, it must be happening for a reason, and that makes me all the more concerned about doing the right thing.'

'I can see that. I can also see that you're under a lot of pressure, making it all the more important that I know what's going on so that I can help you through it. Do you want to leave right away? I can arrange for someone to take over here and see to Mrs Jenkins for you, if you like.'

Katie shook her head. 'No, I need to see the results of the scan for myself. I hate to start treating a patient and then shunt them over to someone else just so I can get out the door.'

'All right. I'll come along and take a look at the

films with you. We'll go along to Radiology now, if you like. It will save time.'

Did he doubt that she was capable of diagnosing her patient's problem? Was he going to double-check her work every time she was under a strain of some sort? She could hardly insist that it wasn't necessary for him to keep tabs on her, though, could she, when he was the one who was in charge of the unit?

She walked with him to the lift. Monica Jenkins was still undergoing the scan when they arrived in the radiology unit, and Sarah was watching from the technician's room where the films were being relayed to a computer monitor. Katie studied them as she stood alongside Alex and the technician.

'There's the problem,' Alex murmured, trailing a finger across the screen. 'It's no wonder the poor woman has a headache.'

'I was half expecting some kind of aneurysm,' Katie said, 'but that's an AVM, isn't it? Do you think it's operable?' An arteriovenous malformation, a mass of abnormal blood vessels, might sometimes be located deep within the brain, but this one looked as though it was relatively accessible.

'It should be, and we need to deal with it right away before it ruptures. We'll bring in a vascular neurosurgeon to do a cerebral angiograph, and then she'll have to go up to Theatre.' He turned to her. 'That was a good call, Katie. I doubt if many people would have picked up on it being something more serious from her symptoms.'

She managed a faint smile. 'I'm thankful that I did.'

Sarah was stunned. 'I never expected to see that. I was convinced that she had a migraine. You must be thrilled to bits to have discovered what was wrong.'

'I think relieved is more the word that I would use,' Katie said.

Sarah's mouth curved. 'Shall I go and call the surgeon now?'

She nodded. 'Yes, please. I'll go and have a word with Mrs Jenkins when she comes out of the scan room. I think she may be a bit shocked by the result. She was still expecting to just be given some stronger painkillers and sent on her way.'

Katie went and spoke to the woman and tried to reassure her about the forthcoming surgery. Staying calm for her patient helped her to get over the underlying worry about Jessica, but she knew that when she left the hospital she had more difficulties to face.

'I imagine that you will be going for surgery very shortly,' she told Monica. 'I'm off duty now, but I'll try to get in to see you some time tomorrow. You've been very brave, but I'm afraid your anniversary celebrations are going to have to be put on hold for a while.'

Monica's husband was waiting for her when she came out of the radiology unit. 'Dr Brooklyn explained to me what was going on,' he said. 'It makes me glad that we came here today. I daren't think what might have happened if we'd just left it.'

Katie gave him a brief smile. 'You did the right thing.'

A short time later she went along the corridor to the

doctors' lounge to retrieve her bag and jacket. She was glad that she had picked up on Monica's problem, but she could so easily have followed another course and treated the woman as though her condition had been less serious. Wasn't this the whole reason that she had decided to leave A and E? Every day she was called on to make life-or-death decisions, and even now she was uneasy about whether she was good enough to make that call.

The sense of disquiet stayed with her as she turned her mind to Jessica and her problems. Somehow she needed to get to the bottom of the situation. She reached for her bag and straightened, trying to gather herself together.

'You look as though you're in a bit of a state,' Alex said. 'Why don't you let me drive you into town? You could always leave your car here overnight and I'll pick you up for work in the morning. It's not out of my way so it would be no problem.'

'I thought you didn't have much sympathy for Jessica and her scrapes. You keep telling me that she's trouble and I would be better off if she wasn't staying with me, so why would you want to help me out?'

'Because I care about you,' he said simply. 'I can see that you aren't going to listen to common sense and send her back home right away, so I suppose I just have to go along with what you're doing and try to support you the best way I can in the meantime. Sooner or later she'll come to realise that she needs to be with her parents and her friends from school.'

But he still wasn't happy to have her around, was he? She looked up at him, her lips wavering a fraction as she tried to stem a small ripple of unease that washed over her. The truth was, she couldn't see a time when Jessica would want to go back to the situation at home.

She was Jessica's lifeline. There had always been a strong bond between the two of them, and she had felt incredibly guilty about leaving her sister behind when she had come to the Lake District. Her one thought back then had been to put the disaster of her hospital experience behind her and make a fresh start.

It hadn't occurred to her that Jessica depended on her so much. She had reasoned that it would be enough to go back and visit on a regular basis, but clearly that hadn't worked out. Perhaps she should never have come here in the first place…and maybe she would have to go back eventually.

'I can manage,' she said huskily.

He slipped his arms around her, enclosing her in his embrace. 'I know that,' he murmured. 'But together we can put it right. I'll help to make you strong. You just need to give me the chance.'

She was still looking up at him, but even so she wasn't ready for his tender kiss when it came. He bent his head towards her and captured her lips, brushing them gently with his own, startling her as every fibre of her being came to vibrant life.

That dreamy, delicate touch was enough to send her nervous system into overload, and in response her mouth softened and clung to his, her body crushed against him so that she was aware of every taut sinew. He looked into her eyes and kissed her again, more deeply this time, sweeping her away on a warm tide of sensation.

His hands gently stroked the length of her body, gliding over her spine and coming to rest lightly on the curve of her hips. 'Let me help you,' he said, his voice rough around the edges. 'We'll sort this out and then I'll take you home.'

'Thank you,' she said softly, giving in. 'I think I'd appreciate that.'

# CHAPTER EIGHT

'DID Jessica give you any idea of what happened?' Alex sent Katie an oblique glance as he drove along the main road towards the town.

'Uh…no, not really.' For the last few minutes Katie had been lost in a world of her own, staring out of the car window at the office buildings and the neat town square. It had all gone by in a haze because she wasn't really conscious of what she was seeing.

Her stomach was in knots, her mind taken up with thoughts of Jessica and what kind of mess she might have landed herself in, but even though she was worried, overriding all that was the memory of Alex's kiss. Katie could still feel the imprint of it on her mouth. It had been so unexpected, and yet so deliciously enticing. Alex's words, though, brought her back to reality with a start. 'She just said that she had been accused of stealing something, but she insisted that she wasn't guilty.'

'Didn't you say that she was in town with her friends?'

'Yes, I did. She's with Sophie and Jade. Apparently they're all being held in a room at the store and the female store detective keeps asking them questions.'

'Do you know the other girls at all?'

'I've met them. They've been to the cottage for tea on a couple of occasions, and they seem like nice girls. I suppose they can be a bit silly at times but I didn't have any problem with them. I've met their parents, too, and they're good people.'

'I expect they will have gone to the store as well. Perhaps between us we can find out what's going on and put it right.'

'I hope so.' She sent him a quick glance. 'I'm glad that you came with me. I would have coped, but it makes me feel better knowing that you're by my side.'

'That was the general idea.' His mouth curved. 'Besides, it might help to face the opposition in force.'

'You were always one to stick up for others, weren't you?' She studied his features as he concentrated on the road ahead. His face was angular, with a strong jaw and a perfectly formed mouth, and even in this simple setting he took her breath away. His large fingers were curled about the steering-wheel, and it occurred to her that they were strong, capable hands. She felt safe, having him near.

She said softly, 'I still can't understand how it is that you turned out to be so strong and steady in your dealings with people. What happened after you left the children's home? I know that you had been in care several times before then, but the foster-homes didn't really work out, did they?'

'I never really fitted in,' he said. 'I suppose that was partly my fault because, to be honest, I resented being there. I felt that I should be at home, taking care of my mother. I didn't feel as though I was a child.'

'Did you go back to your mother?'

'Yes, and we muddled through for a while, but then my aunt came back from overseas, and when she realised what a state my mother was in she decided that she needed to stay in England where she could keep an eye on her. My uncle's work meant that he had to travel around a lot, but Aunt Jane decided to put down roots here again.'

He slowed the car as they came to a junction. 'I think my uncle was happy enough to accept that, and he tried to organise things so that he would be based nearer home from then onwards. In the end Mum and I moved to the Lake District as well. My mother sold the house and bought a small place not far from where my aunt and uncle were living. From my point of view it was great, because they're both lovely people, and they have a son who was like a brother to me.'

Katie smiled. 'I knew there had to be a reason why you were so secure in yourself. Your aunt must have made an appearance in your life just at the crucial moment.'

'I guess she did.'

'Was your aunt the one who tried to get your mother into rehabilitation?'

He nodded. 'Yes, she did. None of the attempts worked out too well because they relied on her to keep to the programme through her own efforts, but I've managed to register her with a residential place that offers various forms of treatment. There's individual counselling and group therapy, along with beautiful surroundings and good food. It's not just short-term rehab to get her off the drugs, but a much longer programme that looks at rebuilding the way she lives her life. I think if she gets the chance to build up her strength and finds new ways of coping with stress, she'll be on the road to recovery.'

'That sounds as though it might be promising. I hope it works out for her…and for you.'

'Thanks.' He gave a brief smile. 'One of the activities they encourage at the centre is gardening. They have greenhouses where the patients can potter about and plots of land that can be prepared for cultivation. I think my mother will enjoy that. It's one hobby where she's always found peace.'

'Well, if she's looking for therapy outside the residential place, she can always come and work in my garden,' Katie said, smiling wryly. 'I'm still trying to cut my way through the brambles.'

He chuckled. 'So if you don't turn up for work one morning, I'll know where to come looking.'

'Too right.' Her smile faded and she tensed as he began to turn the car into a parking space. 'I hadn't realised that we were here already.'

'It doesn't seem too long a journey when you're busy talking, does it?'

'No, it doesn't.' Perhaps that was the reason he had brought her out of her reverie. He must have realised that she was deep in thought and was anxious about her sister. She pulled in a shaky breath. What kind of trouble had Jessica landed herself in? Were her newfound friends leading her astray?

He slid out of the driver's seat and came to open the passenger door. 'Don't worry about it,' he said as she stepped out. 'She's only thirteen and she hasn't been in trouble before. Nothing terrible is going to happen.' He locked the car and sent her a quick, assessing glance.

'That's probably true.' The thought was cheering, and Katie brightened a little.

'Of course it is.' He wrapped his arms around her and pulled her close so that for a moment or two she laid her cheek against his chest and he bent his head to gently nuzzle the silk of her curls.

'Better now?' he asked after a moment or two, and she nodded.

'I'm fine.'

She hurried with Alex into the store where Jessica was being held, and after a short consultation with one of the store personnel they were shown into an upstairs office.

Jessica was sitting on a leather-covered bench seat to one side of the room, but she leapt to her feet and hurried over to Katie as soon as she appeared. 'They've kept us here for ages,' she said tearfully. 'I keep telling them that we didn't mean to do anything wrong, but they won't believe me. I said I'm sorry and I don't know how I came to have the necklace on me.'

Katie frowned. Things didn't look too good, especially if Jessica was admitting having had the property on her. But it didn't make any sense at all. Jessica wasn't the sort of girl to do anything that might get her into trouble with the law.

Jessica's face crumpled. 'The lady phoned Mum. I told her I'm not living there just now, but she wouldn't listen and she went to look up the number. Now I'm going to be in trouble at home as well.'

'Let's not worry about that right now.' Katie saw that Alex had gone to speak to the stony-faced woman who stood at the far side of the room. She put a reassuring arm around her sister's shoulders. 'It's all right, I'm here to look after you. Just go and sit down while I talk to the store detective.'

Jessica did as she suggested and went to sit beside her friends once more. Katie cast a glance at Sophie and Jade, who were both white-faced. 'Are you two in trouble as well?' she asked.

Both girls nodded. 'She said we were all in on it,' Sophie blurted out. 'It wasn't true. We weren't doing anything wrong, but she keeps trying to make us say we stole the necklace.'

'Do your parents know that you're here?'

'Yes,' Sophie said. 'I rang them, and they said they were on their way.'

'That's good. Just stay here and don't say anything while I try to sort this out.' Katie looked at Jade to see if she wanted to add anything to what had been said, but the girl was bending down to adjust her shoe and she decided to leave her be for the moment.

She went to join Alex on the other side of the room.

'This is Mrs Bailey,' he said, introducing the detective. 'She says the girls have been here for an hour. They're accused of taking a necklace.'

'It was in her pocket,' the woman said, waving a hand in Jessica's direction. 'I saw the other girl remove it from the stand earlier and show it to her friend. It was never placed back on the stand. I watched them and saw that none of them went to the cash desk before they headed for the exit. As soon as I saw that they were about to leave, I stopped them. I guessed that one of them must have it.'

She paused to pull in a breath and straighten her back in an authoritative gesture. 'I'm waiting for the manager to return from his meeting. He'll decide whether or not to call the police.'

'Did you see my sister put the necklace into her pocket?' Katie asked.

'No.' The woman hesitated for a moment or two. 'I didn't see that, but they were messing about and one of them must have slipped it in there at some point while I was talking to one of my colleagues.'

Alex was frowning. 'So, let me get this straight. You didn't see Jessica put the necklace into her pocket, and you weren't watching them the whole time?'

'Not the whole time, no. I was distracted for a minute or two…but she had it on her. I made her turn out her pockets and I found it.'

Just then there was a knock on the door and Sophie's parents walked into the room, followed by Jade's mother. Sophie ran over to her father and started to tug at his arm. 'Please, get me out of here,' she said. 'That woman keeps asking us questions, and she doesn't believe anything that we say.'

Jade was struggling to get to her feet. 'What happened?' her mother was asking. 'They said that something had been stolen.'

The girl was limping as she walked over to her mother. 'I was just looking at the necklace,' she said. 'It was on a stand near some stairs that led to the upper level. Jess was coming down from there and I went to show it to her, and then I twisted my foot on one of the steps. I don't really know what happened after that because my ankle was hurting so much. Jess held on to me to stop me from falling and then Sophie came to help me.'

She pulled in a ragged breath. 'We decided that we would go outside and sit down on a bench so that I could rest my foot, but when we were going towards the door this lady came and stopped us. I'd forgotten all about the necklace.'

Jade's mother was looking concerned. 'I think you'd better let me take a look at that ankle. Go and sit back down,' she said. 'I'll help you to your seat.'

Alex shot a look at the girl. 'Did you tell Mrs Bailey that your ankle was hurting?' he asked.

'Yes, but she didn't believe me.'

He turned to Jade's mother, who was watching intently as Jade cautiously tried to take off her shoe. 'I'm a doctor,' he said. 'Would you like me to take a look at the ankle?'

'Would you? Oh, yes, please do.'

Katie came to stand beside him and Jessica looked up at the mother and said, 'My sister's a doctor as well. They both work at the hospital.'

'Shall I help you to take off your sock?' Katie asked, bending down beside the girl.

Jade nodded. 'Is my foot swollen? It feels as though it is. It hurts a lot. Is it broken?'

Alex knelt down and was gently running his fingers over the teenager's foot. 'I don't think so. It's probably a bad sprain,' he said. 'There's quite a lot of swelling and I think you might have torn a ligament, but we probably need to do an X-ray to be sure that there's no fracture.'

Katie went over to Mrs Bailey. 'Do you have a first-aid kit here?' she asked. 'We'll need a stretch bandage and some adhesive tape.'

The woman looked disconcerted. 'Yes, we have one. Are you saying that she really has hurt her ankle? I thought she was making it up.'

'I think you'll be able to see for yourself that the ankle is swollen,' Katie said. 'If you will fetch me the first-aid kit…?'

Mrs Bailey hurried away. When she came back a few minutes later, the manager was with her. He was a middle-aged man, slightly overweight, and he was frowning heavily.

'I'm sorry to hear that the young lady has hurt

herself,' he said. 'You have to understand that we've been having a lot of trouble with teenagers in the store since the holidays began. We have had to start taking a hard line with them. Shoplifters can cost us a lot of money.'

Alex stood up. 'Perhaps you should review your policy with regard to detaining youngsters,' he said. 'It's one thing to apprehend them but quite another to deny them medical care, search them and subject them to questioning without an appropriate adult being present.'

The manager looked uncomfortable. 'We do have the right to detain people if we think they're stealing. Nearly all of them deny that they were doing anything wrong and we sometimes have to take a firm stance.'

Alex wasn't convinced. 'There's a difference between taking a firm stance and being over-zealous.'

'Mrs Bailey was only doing her job,' the man said.

Katie relieved Mrs Bailey of the first-aid kit and began to bind up Jade's ankle. 'This should help to ease it for you until we can get it X-rayed at the hospital,' she said quietly to the girl. 'We'll see to it that you get some painkillers.'

Sophie's father had clearly heard enough. He came over to the manager and said abruptly, 'We're going to take Jade and her mother over to the hospital so that she can get further treatment for the ankle. Sophie will be coming with us. As far as I can tell, this has all been a mistake. My daughter had nothing to do with taking the jewellery and, anyway, I think you've kept all of them here long enough. If you need to talk to us, you can ring us on this number.' He scribbled down a phone number on a piece of paper and the manager looked at it and ran a finger under his collar as if to ease some slight pressure there.

'Yes, well, I expect that in your daughter's case, and her friend's, we can forget about this unfortunate event in this instance. They didn't have any items on them after all.'

Sophie and Jade said goodbye to Jessica and then left the room with their parents. Just as the door was about to close behind them another man appeared in the doorway and Katie looked up to see that her neighbour had arrived.

'Nathan!' Jessica exclaimed, her face lighting up a fraction. 'You're here... You must have got my message after all.'

Nathan nodded. 'I did. I came as soon as I could.'

The manager frowned. 'And you are?'

'Nathan Walker.' He handed him a card. 'I'm Jessica's solicitor.' He glanced across the room at Katie. 'Do you want to tell me what's going on?'

He drew her to one side and she quickly filled him in on the details. Alex, in the meantime, directed a sharp look in the manager's direction.

'Are you actually considering pressing charges where Jessica is concerned?'

The man's expression was strained. 'After all's said and done,' he murmured, 'the necklace was found in the girl's pocket.'

Alex narrowed his eyes. 'I expect that's because it

fell in there when her friend took a tumble. I imagine that they forgot all about it when Jade hurt herself.'

'That's just her version of the story.'

At this point Nathan decided to intervene. He was frowning. 'As I understand it, the girls were apprehended before they left the store. In which case, no theft occurred. You could only accuse them of stealing if they had actually gone outside.'

'But she might have intended to steal it.'

Nathan shrugged. 'You would have to prove that. I doubt if your store's reputation would be served well if it came out in court that you had kept an injured girl here without allowing her treatment. Neither would it enhance your image if it was bandied about that you allow children to be interrogated without a parent or guardian present.'

The manager made an odd coughing sound as he tried to clear his throat. 'We have lots of problems with youngsters, and they seem to think they can run rings round us. We have to be vigilant, and sometimes we have to be tough.'

'Maybe so, but I think you've overstepped the mark this time,' Alex said, his eyes taking on a cool glitter. 'I believe we're done here.' He glanced at Nathan, raising a brow in query.

Nathan nodded confirmation and Alex's jaw hardened as he returned his gaze to the manager. 'Perhaps you should consider fitting an electronic warning system if you want to cut down on the amount of theft you're experiencing.'

He held open the door for the others to pass through, and together they walked out of the store.

'Thanks for that Alex,' Katie said, letting out a sigh of relief when they were back in the fresh air. 'It was wonderful how you handled things. You knew exactly what to do and say.'

She turned to Nathan. 'As for you, it was like a weight lifted off my shoulders when you arrived and underlined the legal situation. I'm so thankful that you came.'

Nathan gave her a hug and pressed his cheek to hers. 'Any time, Katie. You know I would to do anything for you and Jessica.'

Katie smiled up at him. 'You're a treasure. I'm sure Jessica feels the same way.'

'I do,' Jessica said eagerly. 'I was so scared in there. I didn't know whether you would be able to get away from work, but I'm so glad that you did.'

Katie watched the two of them as they chatted. Nathan was a good neighbour to her and she knew that she was lucky to have him around. She glanced up at Alex, a smile still hovering on her lips.

His expression was strangely brooding, though, as he studied Nathan, and she couldn't quite make out what he was thinking. Her smile faded. Was he put out because Nathan had turned up?

She frowned. It wasn't like him to be petty. Alex had handled things with competent ease, and she felt sure that, faced with Alex's opposition, the manager would have dropped any action he might have been considering. It was just that Nathan had the law at his fingertips and he had managed to add his argument and helped to put a swift end to the proceedings. Why would any of that be a problem for Alex?

Katie said carefully, 'Do you remember me telling you about Nathan? He lives next door to us and he helped me out quite a lot when I first moved into the cottage. There were all sorts of things that didn't work properly—the plumbing, the electrical system and so on—and he showed me how to fix them.'

'Yes, I remember. You have breakfast together quite often, you said.' He sent Nathan an assessing look. 'As things turned out, it's fortunate for you that he's a good lawyer, too.'

Nathan lightly squeezed Jessica's shoulder, and then turned back to Katie. 'I managed to find a space in the car park just around the corner. It isn't always easy to find a parking place in town, is it? Are you in your car or do you need a lift back? I wasn't sure whether you would have caught a taxi to bring you here.'

'Alex brought me,' Katie murmured. 'We parked in the same place, so it looks as though we're all headed in the same direction. Perhaps we'll see you back at the cottage? I'll put the kettle on.'

'It's a deal,' Nathan answered.

He was in a jovial mood as he slid behind the wheel of his sports car a short time later. 'See you back home in a few minutes.'

Jessica watched him zoom away as she climbed into Alex's car. 'Talk about burning rubber,' she said. 'Cool car, though.'

Katie smiled. 'Fasten your seat belt,' she murmured. 'I hope you realise how lucky you are, having Alex and Nathan come to your rescue.'

'Yeah, I do. I still don't know why that lady didn't believe us, though.' Her face grew solemn. 'Do you think Jade will be all right?'

Katie nodded. 'Yes, I'm sure she will. They'll give her painkillers at the hospital and make sure that her ankle is comfortable. Like Alex, I'm pretty sure it's not a break.'

Alex started at the engine and drove out of the car park. He wasn't saying anything, just listening to the exchange between Katie and Jessica, and Katie couldn't help wondering if there was something on his mind.

'Will you stay and have some tea with us when we get home?' she asked. 'I prepared Cornish pasties and a fruit salad before work this morning. It would be good if you could come in and share them with us.'

'I don't think so,' Alex said. 'There are things I have to do. Some other time perhaps?' He scanned her features briefly before turning his attention back to the road. He still had that brooding quality about him, as though he was trying to work something out in his mind.

'OK.' Katie was subdued. Something wasn't quite right, but she couldn't work out what it was.

## CHAPTER NINE

KATIE opened her front door to Alex bright and early the next day.

'I'm a bit before time,' he greeted her, 'but I wasn't sure whether we needed to drop Jessica off somewhere before we head for the hospital.'

'Oh, that's all right.' Katie drank in his lightly bronzed features. He was as smartly turned out as ever, wearing a grey suit, the jacket unbuttoned to reveal a blue linen shirt underneath. He appeared to be more relaxed this morning and she was glad of that. 'I've arranged for her to spend the day with my neighbour. After everything that's gone on lately I need to know that she's being looked after.' She waved him inside the cottage. 'Come in. There's some coffee in the pot.'

Alex hesitated. 'She's spending the day with your neighbour?' he echoed.

Katie came to a halt in the narrow hallway. 'She lives just a few houses away,' she explained, 'and she has a daughter who is just a little younger than Jessica. They get on well together.' She gave Alex a long look. 'Did you think I meant Nathan?'

A guarded look came into his eyes. 'That had occurred to me. I don't want to intrude on your breakfast with him.'

'You won't do that. He's already gone off to work. Not that it would have mattered.' She ushered Alex along the hallway. 'Jessica's still in the process of getting herself ready. She's been at it for half an hour, would you believe? I can't imagine that I used to take that long when I was her age.'

Alex laughed. 'Neither can I. You're beautiful enough without needing any extra help.'

Katie's eyes widened. 'Compliments this early in the morning? That can't be bad.' He was certainly in a better mood today. Whatever had caused him to be so deep in thought yesterday had obviously dissolved overnight.

She showed him into the kitchen and started to pour coffee. 'Sit down,' she told him. 'I'll just finish clearing away these breakfast dishes. I seem to have been at sixes and sevens ever since last night. There's been one thing after another going on, what with visits from Sophie and Jade's parents…and then my mother phoned. I don't seem to have had a minute to myself.'

'How is Jade? If they hadn't all dashed off, I would have taken her to the hospital myself.'

'Yes, I told them that we would have been happy to do that, but I think they were anxious to make their escape. She's fine. Colin examined her and came to the same conclusion as you—that it was a bad sprain. She'll have to rest up for a while and put ice packs on the ankle.'

He gave her a querying look. 'I'm assuming that the parents have no worries about what happened. They believe that the girls were telling the truth.'

'Yes, of course.' She frowned, staring at him. 'Do you have any doubts?'

He shook his head. 'No, I think it was as the girls said. They forgot all about the necklace and it must have slipped into Jessica's pocket.' He swallowed his coffee. 'How is Jessica this morning? She seems to have been off key quite a bit lately.'

'Well, it didn't help that my mum and dad called. They were both worried about what was going on. I think they must have realised for the first time in a while that she's just a child and she needs them to be there for her. So perhaps it wasn't all bad.'

Alex put his cup down. 'Does that mean that she'll be going home?'

'I don't think so. Not yet, at any rate. She's beginning to realise that she misses them, but she still seems to want to be with me, and it looks as though the only way she'll be content to go home is if I decide to go back there with her.'

He lifted a dark brow. 'Is that likely to happen?'

A cloud came over Katie's features. 'I suppose it will depend on how things go when my contract comes to an end. I'll have to think things through. The thing is,

I've come to learn that I do need to have my family close by. They might bicker and cause me grief, but they are my flesh and blood when all's said and done.'

His eyes darkened. 'I thought perhaps you were becoming stronger and more independent since you've been on your own. When you first came to work at South Lake you were a little uncertain, but you've been gaining in confidence ever since then. I don't know what happened to set you back before you came here, but I think it's been good for you, working in A and E.'

Katie finished stacking crockery in the dishwasher and started to wipe down the kitchen surfaces. She hesitated momentarily.

'I was doing a six-month stint in the surgical specialty connected to A and E,' she said. 'I thought I was doing OK.' She might have said more but Jessica came into the kitchen just then and stopped in her tracks when she saw Alex sitting by the kitchen table.

'Oh,' she said. 'I thought I heard the doorbell. Have you come to take Katie to work?'

'That's right. She left her car at the hospital yesterday because I thought she might want some company if she was going over to the store.'

Jessica made a grimace. 'I'm sorry about that. I'm sorry that I caused so much trouble. I didn't mean to do it.' She sent him a quick, diffident look. 'You stood up for me,' she said. 'Thank you for doing that.'

Alex smiled. 'You're welcome.'

Jessica looked uncertain for a moment, and then mumbled, 'I'd better go and get my bag if I'm going to

Sue's house for the day. She said that she would take me and Charlotte out to a country park.'

She spun out of the room and Katie heard her padding about upstairs a few seconds later. She sent Alex a grin. 'Her whole life is a race against time. I thought working in A and E was frantic, but she makes my head spin sometimes.'

He laughed and got to his feet, coming around the table to her. 'Maybe you should slow down a little and take time to enjoy the here and now.'

She looked at him quizzically. 'What does that mean?'

His hands slid around her waist, his palms flattening on her rib cage as he drew her towards him. 'It means that I really, really want to kiss you. I want to take away the worry of everyday life and kiss you until you have that dreamy look that comes over your face when your head is off in the clouds somewhere. Like this…'

And he did exactly that, capturing her lips and tantalising her with a kiss that made the world shift beneath her feet and rock on its axis. He moved his hands over her curves so that her body melted beneath his touch and meshed with his, and her limbs became weak and insubstantial. Then his fingers traced a path over the soft swell of her breast, and her senses leapt in a fiery explosion of delicious response. A husky moan sounded in her throat.

She kissed him in return, her hands gliding over the hard wall of his chest and moving upwards so that her fingers tangled in the silky hair at the back of his head. She wanted him, urgently, desperately, needing the fierce passion of his kiss to go on and on.

There was a clatter, though, followed by the sound of pounding feet as Jessica headed down the stairs once more, and reluctantly he dragged his lips away from hers.

Katie's mind was in a whirl, her thoughts in a far-off place, a mist of feverish desire clouding her gaze.

'Are you OK?' Alex was studying her through half-closed eyes, his expression faintly amused.

'Oh, yes,' she managed in a breathless whisper. 'Oh, yes, I'm fine.'

He moved away from her as Jessica came into the room.

'Are we ready to go now?' he asked, turning to look at her sister and shielding Katie with his body at the same time. It amazed her that he could be so calm and casual and so very much in control of himself.

Jessica gave them both an odd look. 'I'm ready when you are,' she said, as though she had been waiting for ages.

At the hospital, Katie worked her way through her list of patients and didn't see very much of Alex. He was working with Colin, attending to people who had been injured in a car crash, while she was dealing with suspected stroke cases, back injuries and a patient with a virulent chest infection.

At break-time she went to see how Monica Jenkins was doing after her operation, which had removed the distended blood vessels that had caused her so much trouble.

The woman was drowsy from the after-effects of surgery and medication, but she appeared to have come through everything without a hitch.

'I'm glad to see that you're doing so well,' Katie told her. 'The nurse tells me that you're going to stay here for a week or so, but you should soon be back on your feet. Perhaps you'll be able to have a delayed anniversary party when you're back at home.'

Monica smiled. 'My husband says he'll take us all out to celebrate. That will be so much easier.'

'That's probably a good idea.'

Katie went back to A and E. It was as frantic as ever, and there was still no sign of Alex.

'I think he had to go for a meeting with management,' Sarah said. 'I know they are going to make up their minds any time now about who is to head up the new unit. I hope it works out well for him. I know how much he wants that job.'

'I'm sure he would be the best person to run it,' Katie said. 'He's certainly made everything run smoothly here.'

She hurried out to the ambulance bay where the paramedics were bringing in a young man who was having difficulty breathing. He was in his twenties and appeared to have a problem with his throat. The paramedic explained that the tissues of the throat were swollen and seemed to be compromising his airway.

'We have him on oxygen,' the paramedic said. 'He's feverish, with neck pain and referred ear pain. He has tachycardia, heart rate 110, and he's showing signs of dehydration. He is finding it difficult to talk, but he said the throat pain came on about four days ago.'

'Thanks. I'll take a look at him.' Katie could see that the young man was agitated and in a state of extreme distress. He was struggling for air. She called for Sarah to assist, and together they wheeled him into the treatment room.

Katie made a quick general examination, looking carefully at his throat. 'It's very inflamed,' she murmured to Sarah, who had come to assist. 'There appears to be a large abscess, which is probably causing most of his problems. I'm going to have to aspirate it urgently, otherwise he's not going to be able to breathe at all.'

Katie explained the situation to the young man. 'We'll spray your throat with an anaesthetic and add painkillers so that you shouldn't be too uncomfortable while we drain the abscess,' she told him. 'I'm going to do a blood test and we'll send a culture from your throat to the lab so that we know what type of infection we are dealing with. In the meantime, I'll get you started on antibiotics.'

Sarah hurried to prepare a trolley for the procedure. 'Will you be using a 19-gauge needle?' she asked.

'Yes, with a 10 cc syringe, and I'll need 4 cc of lidocaine with epinephrine. I'll have to put in an intravenous line for fluids, and he'll need steroids as well, once I've finished, to help combat the inflammation. Would you give Anaesthesiology and Otolaryngology a call in case I need any emergency assistance? I can't afford to delay starting the procedure.'

'I'll do that right away.'

Katie worked carefully to drain the abscess. It was essential not to insert the needle too deeply, otherwise there was a risk of piercing the carotid artery.

Keeping a steady hand, she completed the aspiration and Sarah collected the culture that was to be taken to the laboratory. Katie quickly filled in the forms.

'You should start to feel better soon, now that the pressure in your throat has been relieved,' she told her patient.

He briefly closed his eyes in acknowledgement and mouthed the word, 'Thanks.'

Katie turned around, getting ready to leave the treatment room. She saw that Alex was standing in the doorway, and her mouth began to curve into a smile. It faded as soon as she realised that his expression was grim.

'Is something wrong?' she asked.

'Yes, I'm afraid so. I need to talk to you,' he said. 'In my office.'

A shiver ran through her as she went over to him. 'What's happened? Is it Jessica? Is she all right?'

'She's fine,' he said abruptly. He didn't add anything more but turned to walk in the direction of his office. Katie followed him, her mind buzzing with questions.

Once inside his office, Alex shut the door.

Katie stared at him. 'What's this all about?' Had he been told that he wasn't going to be given the promotion he so desperately wanted?

'Perhaps you should sit down,' he suggested. Katie remained standing, and he went on, 'We've had a letter from the hospital where you used to work.'

A knot formed in Katie stomach. After all this time, just when she thought she was in the clear, was the whole horrible incident coming back to haunt her once again?

Alex's glance went over her briefly. 'It appears that one of your former patients is launching a complaint against you. He's consulting with a firm of solicitors with a view to taking you to court.'

Katie's legs felt as though they were crumbling beneath her. Blindly, she fumbled for the arm of a chair and awkwardly sat down.

Alex was quiet, waiting, but when she didn't say anything, he said briskly, 'You were expecting this, weren't you?'

'I wasn't sure. There was a problem, but I didn't know whether it would come to anything.' She stared up at him. 'What is the patient complaining about? What charges is he bringing?'

'He wants to sue for malpractice. He claims that he was injured as a result of surgery that you carried out on him. He's asking for compensation for the stress that he endured and the time that he was unable to work as a result of that injury.'

His gaze pierced her like a laser. 'Why on earth didn't you warn me? As it is, I have management telling me that I need to suspend you while this is investigated. They want to know how it was that none of this came up when you were employed here. I knew nothing about it, so how could I possibly defend you?'

Katie swallowed hard. 'I'm sorry. I hoped that it

wouldn't come to this. I thought it was going to be all right, and I thought that because he had signed a permission form I would be covered against any possible action.'

'Well, it isn't all right, by any means. He's saying that the event occurred because you carried out a procedure you weren't qualified to do.'

'No, that's right, I wasn't.' Katie was shaking inside. Her whole world had collapsed about her, and Alex was looking at her in a way that he had never done before. His mouth made a straight line and his jaw was clenched. There was no way that she could repair the damage.

'Do I have to leave right now?' Her gaze flickered. 'Will I be allowed to do any kind of work within the hospital?'

'All I can tell you is that the hospital chiefs are taking a hard line about any kind of complaint or misdemeanour that they hear about. They worry about meeting targets and the reputation of the hospital, and they have to be sure that any doctor who works here is competent. People are too conscious of league tables nowadays. Everyone has to be whiter than white.'

'I can understand that.' Katie pressed her lips together to stop them from trembling. 'Are they doubting your judgement in taking me on?'

Alex didn't answer. 'That isn't the point right now.'

'Isn't it?' She looked up at him, her blue eyes troubled, her mind numb. 'I didn't mean this to happen,' she said in a choked voice. 'I know how much your promotion means to you, and I can't bear to think that I might have set it back. Believe me, I didn't think it would come to this.'

'It's too late for regrets now. Tell me what happened.' His features were hard edged, and his whole demeanour was tense.

Katie passed her tongue over her dry lips. 'My patient was very ill and I suspected that he was suffering from a pulmonary embolism. I called on my consultant for help, but he wasn't available so I asked the registrar what I should do. He said we would do a pulmonary angiography and he told me that if there was a large blockage to the artery we would try to remove it or disperse it.'

She pulled air into her lungs and tightened her hands to stop them from shaking. 'We took the man up to Theatre and we managed to find the embolism. It was removed successfully and the registrar was instructing me throughout the process. We were both watching the monitor as I manoeuvred the catheter. Everything seemed to be going well, but as I was preparing to withdraw the catheter I saw what looked like an aneurysm in the blood vessel. I thought perhaps it had occurred because the patient had been hypertensive and perhaps that had weakened the artery wall.'

She hesitated for a moment, trying to calm herself. Having to tell him about what had happened brought the memory of those events back to her in full force, and the horror of the situation even now was enough to make her feel weak and faint. 'I'm not sure exactly what happened next, but I think the lights in the theatre failed for a moment or two. There was a major storm outside and we had been experiencing a few problems, but then the generator kicked in.'

She pressed her lips together, flattening them against her lower teeth. 'The next thing I knew, my patient was bleeding from a rupture in the artery. I was trying to stem the blood flow, but I wasn't getting anywhere, and Helen, the nurse who was assisting, was telling me that the patient had gone into cardiac arrest.'

'What was the registrar doing while all this was going on?'

'He had turned away. He had his back to me and he seemed to be unwell. Then he collapsed. Apparently he was suffering from appendicitis at the time. He'd had pain for some weeks but he'd ignored it, thinking it was just a rumbling abdominal problem that would go away.' She winced. 'It was just unfortunate that it chose that moment to become acute.'

'So what did you do?'

'I asked one of the theatre nurses to go and call for help, both for the registrar and for my patient, while I did what I could to resuscitate the man on the table. It was a massive bleed, and I had to send for blood to transfuse him. I was afraid I was going to lose him.'

'Those kinds of haemorrhages are fatal, more often than not.' Alex's eyes had darkened, and he was watching her intently. 'But your patient is still around to tell the tale. How did you stop the bleeding in the end?'

'I did a transcatheter embolisation, using coils of wire to support the walls of the artery.'

'How on earth were you able to do that? I'm surprised you had the skills.'

Katie's mouth made an odd shape. 'So was I. I'd watched other surgeons do it before that, because I was particularly interested in that aspect of surgery. I'd thought at one time that I might want to specialise, but after what happened that day I didn't want to see a theatre again.'

'I should think that's hardly surprising. I can't imagine how you coped.'

'Neither can I, to be honest. It was nerve-wracking because it was such a horrendous bleed, and I had a struggle to prevent the haemorrhage from causing problems with his other lung. It was a nightmare from start to finish.'

Alex had started to pace the floor. 'So, because of the cardiac arrest and because the patient lost a lot of blood, he had to stay in hospital for much longer than he might have done originally?'

Katie nodded. 'We had to ensure that his blood pressure remained stable as well. His relatives knew from the first that something was wrong because he was in Theatre for much longer than expected.'

She sent him a worried glance. 'What happens now? Will there be an investigation? These things take a long while to sort out, don't they?'

'They may do.' He pulled in a sharp breath and straightened as though he had come to a decision. 'Look, Katie, I'm going to have to get reports from various people who were involved. It's management policy that you won't be able to carry out any of your normal duties here until we've resolved this, and it depends on how they view things as to whether you'll be allowed to carry out other tasks. What I suggest you do is take a few days' leave. I'll let you know as soon as I have anything positive to tell you.'

'All right.' Her mouth wavered with uncertainty. 'I'll get my things together.' She made an attempt at a smile. 'I suppose there's one good thing to come out of this—Jessica will be pleased to have me at home with her.' She frowned. 'And I suppose it will give me time to look through the job vacancy columns.'

'Let's wait and see what happens before you do that, shall we?'

'I'd say the odds were stacked against me, wouldn't you? I performed procedures that I wasn't qualified to do without supervision, and the patient seems to be saying that I caused the rupture of the artery in the first place. I don't think that's true, but I can't prove it.'

'Even so, it may not come to a court case if we can sort this out at a local level.'

He was being as encouraging as he could in the circumstances, and Katie appreciated that. She was thoughtful as she made her way towards the door.

'But if it does… Nathan said he might be able to help me if there was a problem. I suppose I could ask him if there's anything he could do. He might know a specialist lawyer who could act for me.'

Alex looked at her with narrowed eyes. 'You told him about it?'

Katie nodded miserably. 'It sort of came up when I first moved into the house and was still pretty much preoccupying me. I've been trying to push it to the back of my mind ever since. I know that I ought to have told you, but I was hoping that as nothing further had happened, it would all go away.'

'These things never go away. You're right, you should have told me so that I could have been prepared for all of this. Now all I can do is try to mop up the mess.' He frowned. 'As to Nathan, I believe your former hospital will provide their own lawyers if it becomes necessary.'

He started to gather up papers from the table and Katie hesitated, her fingers resting on the handle of the door. 'Will you call me and let me know if there's any news?'

'Of course. Go home, Katie. I'll do what I can to put this right.'

Katie went to the doctors' lounge and started to collect her belongings. He hadn't said anything about his hopes for promotion, but she guessed they had been dashed. It was all her fault, and she didn't know how to make amends.

Things had started off so well that morning, and she still remembered the way he had made her feel when he had taken her into his arms and kissed her. It had been as though she belonged there. Her mouth began to tremble. He wouldn't want her now. She had ruined everything for him, and his faith in her had gone.

# CHAPTER TEN

'IT ISN'T fair.' Jessica was frowning heavily. She was sitting at the kitchen table, trying to fit the pieces of a jigsaw puzzle together. 'I don't see how they can blame you and say you hurt the man when you saved his life.'

'I don't think the hospital managers see it quite that way,' Katie said. She had finished ironing the last few items from her laundry basket, and now she was getting ready to put the clothes away. She sighed. 'At least now I have plenty of time to do all these chores,' she said.

The doorbell sounded, and Jessica got to her feet. 'I'll answer it. Do you think it will be Alex?'

Katie's heart gave a sudden lurch before settling back into its normal rhythm once more. 'I shouldn't think so.'

Alex had given her a call just the day before to say that he had spoken to the registrar who had been in Theatre with her and asked him to give him a written account of what had happened. He was trying to get in touch with Helen, the nurse who had assisted her, but so far he hadn't had any luck in finding her.

'You said that she was young and single,' he had said. 'I suppose there's a possibility that she might have married. Do you have any idea as to whether she was involved with someone?'

'There was a doctor who worked in the renal unit. I know that they were very close. I've already tried to find her, but she must have moved on to another hospital. She said she wanted to specialise in paediatrics.'

'I'll see what I can do.'

Alex's tone had been brisk, and he would have rung off there and then, except that Katie said quickly, 'I was thinking of taking Jessica into town tomorrow. Would you like to meet us at the pizza house near the hospital? I thought perhaps we could talk for a while.'

'I can't do that, Katie. I've several meetings set up, and then I have to go away for a couple of days or so. I'll give you a ring when I get back, if you like.'

'Yes, that would be fine.' Katie was disappointed. She wasn't going to hold her breath. He hadn't given her any clue as to where he was going, and she remembered that he had some leave due. Perhaps he was going to take that break by the coast that he had talked about some time ago.

The thought bothered her more than she could have imagined. She desperately wanted him to be here by her side, and she longed for the sound of his deep, warm voice, soothing her worries away, but none of that was going to happen, was it? He may have kissed her and held her close, but all that was over now, wasn't it? She had let him down and things would never be the same again.

'Katie…look. You'll never guess who's here…' Jessica's voice was filled with surprise and more than a hint of excitement, so that Katie came out of her reverie and looked over to where she was standing by the door to the kitchen.

'Mum…Dad,' she said, her eyes widening. She put down the cotton top that she had been folding and went to greet them. 'I had no idea you were planning on coming over here.'

'Well, we thought we would come and see how you were both doing.' Katie's mother was smiling as she gave her a hug. 'Jessica rang to tell us what had happened at the hospital, and we thought you might need a bit of support.' She ran a hand through her thick brown hair, tucking it back behind her ears. 'We booked ourselves into a hotel just a little way from here. I know you don't have a lot of room in the cottage.'

'I'm sure I could have managed to squeeze you in somehow. It's lovely to see you both.' Katie gave her stepfather a warm embrace. 'Are you sure you can spare the time to be away from work? I know how busy you are.'

'That's the thing…work has always been my driving force, and it doesn't seem to have brought me anything but stress.' He looked down at her, and she could see that there were flecks of silver in his hair and lines of strain around his eyes. 'We've been able to have a lot of long chats about things, your mother and I, over the last few weeks, and we've come to the conclusion that perhaps there's more to life than constant struggle. We have some savings put by, and if I take the redundancy being offered we thought we might try our hand at running our own business. It might be less stressful.'

Katie was astonished. 'I can't believe I'm hearing this. Come and sit down, both of you, and tell me all about it.' At least having her parents here would help to take her mind off her troubles for a while.

'I'll put the kettle on, shall I?' Jessica asked.

'That's a good idea.'

Over the next few hours Katie and Jessica sat and talked with their parents. It was strange, but there seemed to be something different about both of them. Her mother was much more relaxed and her stepfather was more animated than she had seen him in a long time. They hadn't decided yet what kind of business they would run, and they were more anxious to talk about any worries that Katie and Jessica had.

A couple of days later they were getting ready to return home. 'If you're not working at present,' her mother said, 'why don't you both come back home and spend a few days with us?'

'I think I'd like that,' Katie answered. She glanced at Jessica, who was nodding in agreement. 'It might give me the break I need, and it will be good for Jess to see her friends again. I can always keep in touch with the hospital by phone if there's anything I need to deal with.'

It didn't take her long to pack for the trip…all she needed was a couple of changes of clothes and her make-up bag.

The journey seemed to take no time at all, and as she approached the broad sweep of the mouth of the Humber, it was as though she had never been away. Settling back into her old house with her parents and Jessica gave Katie an oddly nostalgic sensation, but above all it gave her the time out that she needed.

Jessica went to call on her friends, and looked happy to be home. Katie was pleased for her.

Throughout the weekend that she stayed in her parents' home, Katie tried not to think about what was going on elsewhere. There were no calls from Alex, and she began to accept that he might want to distance himself from her.

'You miss him, don't you?' Jessica said.

'Yes, I do.'

'Have things gone wrong between you?'

'Sort of.'

'Is it because of me?'

Startled, Katie looked at her sister and saw the uncertainty in her eyes. 'No, Jess. What makes you think it was because of you?'

Jessica gave an awkward shrug. 'I know how you like each other, but I was afraid that if you and he were too close…there would be no room for me. I know I wasn't always nice to him. I didn't really mean to turn him off you. I just…I was afraid that you wouldn't want me around any more.'

Katie gave her sister a hug. 'I'll always want you around, Jess, believe me. You're my sister, and you mean the world to me. I'm always going to be there for you, even if you're living here and I'm in the Lake District. You only have to call.'

'You mean it?'

'I mean it.'

Jessica gave a little sigh of contentment. 'I do like him, and he was really good to me. He will come back to you, won't he?'

'Maybe.' Katie daren't think about the alternative. What if she had lost him for ever?

She tried to turn her mind away from melancholy thoughts. Instead, she helped her parents to work through ideas for their new venture, and watched as Jessica began to relax in their company once more. There seemed to have been a general change for the better all around.

On Monday, Katie was ready to go back and face her difficulties once more.

'Will you be happy to stay on here?' she asked Jessica. 'I'll come and see you next week, and we can perhaps arrange for you to come and stay with me again for a while, if you'd like that.'

'That's great,' Jessica said with a smile. 'Yes, I'll be fine. I'd like to meet up with Sophie and Jade again, though, soon.'

'We'll sort something out,' Katie promised.

Back at the cottage, everything seemed strangely quiet. She had become used to having her sister around, but now there was only stillness and a hollow echo that followed her as she moved about the place.

The phone rang, and Katie gave a startled jump.

Could that be Alex, wanting to talk to her? Her pulse quickened.

It wasn't him. Instead, a woman's voice came over the line, and she introduced herself as someone who ran the rehabilitation centre where Alex's mother was staying.

'I know this is an unusual request,' Dr Barstow said, 'but I wonder if you would have the time to speak to Mrs Brooklyn? She's been staying with us for a while. I realise that the two of you have never met before, but she heard that you were a colleague of her son, and it would help her enormously if you would talk to her for a while. It's one of the strands of our rehabilitation process that we suggest our clients have contacts with people who might be able to help with certain aspects of their care. It would only be a question of chatting to her. There needn't be any other involvement.'

Katie frowned. Alex's mother wanted to talk to her? Why would she want to do that?

'Yes, I think that would be all right,' Katie murmured. 'Actually, though, it would probably be better if I were to come and see you. Alex has told me briefly about your centre, and I would be quite interested to see how you work.'

'That would be excellent,' the woman answered, giving her the address and directions. 'I'll look forward to seeing you. I'll let Mrs Brooklyn know that you'll be by tomorrow.'

Katie stared down at the phone when she replaced the receiver. Why wasn't Alex calling her? Where was he?

Would he mind if she were to go and speak to his mother?

The residential centre was just a few miles away from where Katie lived, nestled in a wooded valley overlooking a small lake. It was an old building, set back among trees, with a wide sweep of lawn to the front and shrub gardens to each side.

Dr Barstow met her in the wide hallway at the front of the building and showed her into a spacious room, where glass doors led out onto a large patio. 'It's really good of you to come out here to see us,' she said. 'Mrs Brooklyn…Hannah…is making really good progress. I think being able to talk to you will help her along tremendously.'

Katie glanced around the room. A couple of people were in there, talking to one another, while a nurse stood over by a window, preparing hot drinks.

'Hannah is out on the terrace,' Dr Barstow said. 'I'll take you to her and I'll arrange for some tea to be brought out to you.'

'Thank you.'

Alex's mother was sitting by an ornate white table, taking in the fresh air. She was arranging flowers in a bowl, carefully clipping the stems and inserting each delicate bloom into plastic foam.

Having made the introductions, Dr Barstow left them alone together.

'That looks beautiful,' Katie said, admiring the design Hannah was working on. 'You clearly have talent, to be able to do something like that.'

'It's something that I've learned since I've been staying here,' Hannah said. 'They have such lovely gardens, and they allow me to go and pick whatever flowers I want.'

'That sounds like a dream come true. I'm still struggling to get most of my shrubs tamed into shape, let alone produce flowers.' Katie's mouth curved. 'Would it be all right if I sit with you?'

'Please, do.' Hannah smiled, a sweet, gentle smile that softened her features and brought a glimmer of light into her grey-blue eyes. She had dark, almost black hair that had been trimmed in neat layers to softly frame her face. 'I'm so glad that you came to see me. Alex has told me so much about you.'

'Has he?' Katie was surprised at that.

Hannah nodded. 'He said that you and he met years ago, when you were both staying at the children's home. He was so pleased to have met up with you again.' Her gaze moved over Katie. 'He told me that you were working together, but when he came to see me a few days ago he said that you were in trouble, and that his managers wanted him to suspend you. You must be feeling very unhappy about that.'

Katie wasn't sure how much of the detail Alex had told his mother. She said cautiously, 'It came as a shock. I had hoped that things would work out all right in the end, but they didn't. I know that Alex was hoping to be given the job of taking charge of the new unit, and he wanted everything to run smoothly so that the hospital chiefs would see that he was doing a good job. I'm not sure how much any of this would have set him back.'

'That wasn't exactly what I was concerned about,' Hannah said. 'Alex pretty much takes charge of his own life, and doesn't rely on what other people do or don't do. I feel he does that because I let him down so much over the years.' Hannah grimaced. 'I know he has the idea that you might decide that it's all too much for you to handle and that you'll give in and go back home to where you used to live.'

'I must admit that thought did cross my mind.'

'You shouldn't do that.' Hannah looked into Katie's eyes. 'I know it's not my place to say, but it's the sort of thing I used to do before I came here. My coping strategy was to pretend that bad things weren't happening and that I could hide myself under the covers, so to speak. Since I've been here, I've learned that it's far better to face up to problems. You hide because you think that they're going to overwhelm you but, in fact, hiding makes them worse. It's the fear of the unknown that brings you down. I'm beginning to learn that it's easier to deal with troubles straight on.'

Katie nodded. 'I know what you mean. When I was working at the other hospital and everything started to go wrong, I just ran away. I was still doing that when Alex found me.'

Hannah nodded. 'He said that your sister was going through a bad time, and that you helped her just by being there for her.' She gave a wistful smile. 'That's how it was with my sister, Jane. She went away for quite a long time and I felt lost and alone, but then she came back to me and put me back on my feet. She was brilliant with Alex, too. She made up for all the troubles I'd put him through.'

'He must love you a great deal to have brought you here.' Katie watched as Hannah added sprigs of flowers to fill out the design she was working on. 'This seems to be a wonderful place.'

'It is. They've taught me so much about how to cope with stress. It was hard for me at first because they put so many challenges in front of me, but I didn't have any option but to get through them. It seemed tough to begin with. It was worth it, though. I feel so much stronger for learning how to deal with things, and I can see now where I was going wrong. They've made it clear that I'll always have someone to counsel me if need be when I leave here.' She smiled. 'I'm not going to let Alex down. Things are going to be different from now on.'

Somehow, Katie believed her. 'I'm glad about that.'

'So how will you handle this threat of suspension? Have you worked out what you might do? Do you think you'll go back to where you used to live?'

Katie shook her head. 'No. I like it here in the Lake District. My cottage is small, but it's home for the time being, and I'm going to make the best of it. I'm not running away again. In my heart, I don't believe I did anything wrong, and I'm going to say that to whoever will listen. No matter what happens, I'm going to stand my ground.'

'Good for you.'

They talked for a little while longer, and Katie realised that she could grow fond of Alex's mother. She seemed to have been through a lot, but now she was at a turning point in her life.

'Would it be all right if I come to see you again?' Katie asked when she was getting ready to leave.

'I'd like that,' Hannah said. 'I'd like it very much.'

Katie made her way back to the cottage and tried to work out what it was that had prompted Alex's mother to call her. She hadn't asked for anything for herself or told her much of Alex's thoughts, and yet somehow Katie felt that Hannah had acted purely out of a desire to ensure her son's well-being. How could Katie do anything to help him get what he wanted, except to accept the suspension that management wanted him to impose?

The cottage was silent when she let herself in through the front door, and she wandered into the living room and opened up the French doors into the garden to let the fresh air flow through.

She checked her answering machine to see if there had been any messages, and to her surprise there was one from Alex.

'I've been trying to ring you over the last few days.' His deep voice came from the speaker, and for a moment it was as though he was in the room with her. Her breath caught in her throat until she looked around and realised he was not there. Then her spirits sank. 'Where have you been?' he said. 'I should have asked you for your new mobile number, shouldn't I? Call me?'

No wonder he hadn't rung. She'd forgotten that she had bought herself a new phone and donated the old one to charity. Had he been trying to get in touch all the time she had been at her parents?

She dialled his number. Would he still be at work, or away at the coast? He didn't answer, and she left a voicemail message, telling him that she was at the cottage. She left her mobile number, too, just in case.

He didn't return her call, and after a while she went out into the garden to gather some flowers. There weren't many to choose from, but the roses were in bloom and their scent was enchanting and would cheer her up.

She set them out in a crystal rose bowl, and then went to flick the switch on the coffee-machine. Why didn't Alex ring?

There was a knock at the door, and she guessed it was Nathan, coming to ask for an update on the malpractice suit.

'At last.' Alex was standing there in her porch and he gave her a wry smile. 'Does nothing work around here? It looks as though your doorbell is on the blink, as well as your phone being out of action. Remind me to check the battery for you.'

'Alex?' Katie's eyes widened. 'You're here. You're not at the coast?'

'I was never at the coast. Whatever gave you that idea? Do I get to come in?'

She stared at him, trying to get her head together. 'Of course.' She stood to one side and waited for her heart to stop fluttering.

He shut the door behind him and began to walk along the hallway. 'I had to go to a conference in Yorkshire,' he said. 'I could hardly get out of it because I was one of the speakers.'

'Oh, I see.'

'Hmm.' He looked at her. 'I'm not sure that you do. Shall we go into the kitchen or the living room?'

'The living room,' she said. 'It smells better in there.'

He sent her an odd look. 'I beg your pardon?'

'It's the flowers,' she explained. 'I just brought some in from the garden.'

'Does that make a difference?'

'Well, of course it does. They make the room a much more pleasant place, so that we can sit and talk.'

He shook his head briefly, as though he was trying to clear an irritating fog from it. 'Obviously it must be a woman thing—though I don't think you're quite yourself, are you?' he asked softly.

'Possibly not. It's been a trying time lately.'

'Yes, I know. That's what I wanted to talk to you about. Are you going to come and sit down?' He indicated the sofa, and she went to join him there.

'I found the nurse, Helen,' he said. 'The one who was in Theatre with you.'

'You did?'

'That's right. She married the doctor from the renal unit, and now she's working in the paediatric department at a hospital some ten miles away from your original one. She said she remembered what happened, but better than that she had the presence of mind to save the film of the angiograph and made sure that it would be available if it was ever needed. She said you were too concerned with taking care of the patient to think about doing that.'

'That's probably going to be useful if it should go to court. It will show the rupture quite clearly, won't it?' Her mouth made a downward turn. 'But I guess you're still going to have to suspend me anyway, till it's all sorted one way or the other. When will that begin—right away?'

He frowned. 'Who said anything about suspending you?'

'You did.' Her lips made a straight line. 'You said management told you to suspend me.'

He lifted dark brows. 'I was never going to suspend you.'

She frowned. 'But your promotion—you want to head up the new unit. Has that gone to someone else?'

'I could always have gone for promotion somewhere else. I was never going to follow what management said...not without just cause, and this wouldn't have been just, would it? We can't have people ousted on rumour and conjecture, can we? What we need is an open policy, where people feel free to admit that they're only human and that they can only do their best under difficult circumstances.'

'But the patient complained...'

'Katie, you didn't do anything wrong. Your former registrar gave me permission to view the films from the angiography and they show quite clearly that there was an aneurysm that must have formed independently of what you were doing. It had most likely been there for some time, and it ruptured without any intervention from you, because the artery wall had ballooned and was too thin to sustain the patient's high blood pressure. You didn't cause it to happen. You didn't make any mistakes.'

'I didn't?' She let out a long, slow breath. After all this time, she finally knew the truth.

'Anyway, even if you had, the patient had signed a form agreeing to the procedure, and that kind of operation is never without risk.'

'Yes, but I was a senior house officer. I wasn't experienced enough to do it without supervision…isn't that what he's saying?'

'True, but how would that stand up in court when your consultant had turned off his pager and your registrar was sick? Would he have been happy if you'd simply stood back and let him bleed to death while you waited for a supervisor? Hardly. Once we lay the facts out for the patient and his lawyer, I'm certain that he'll drop the complaint.'

His mouth twisted. 'Your consultant must have been worried that he would be criticised for not being available. It's no wonder he quietly let you go when your contract ended. By seeming to put you in the wrong, it saved him from being embarrassed.'

Katie looked at him in bemusement. 'I thought you blamed me for all this. You were angry with me, and you sent me home. I felt terrible because I thought I had ruined everything for you.'

He reached for her, cupping her shoulders with his palms. 'I was taken aback because you hadn't told me any of it. I thought you didn't trust me enough to confide in me, and that disturbed me more than anything. Of course I didn't blame you, and there's no way you ruined anything for me. I stand by the decisions I make.' His hands were warm on her, gliding over the silk of her bare arms and thrilling her with his touch.

'I was so unhappy,' she said huskily, 'not just about the complaint, but because I thought I'd lost you. You seemed so distant. I didn't know how I was going to be able to go on.'

He looked into her eyes. 'Does that mean you care about me…just a little?'

She gave a choked laugh. 'More than just a little,' she said softly. 'I love you, Alex. I think I've always loved you.'

He wrapped his arms around her and held her as though he wouldn't ever let her go. He bent his head and rested his cheek against hers, his fingers tangling in the softness of her curls. 'I thought you were in love with that lawyer,' he said in a roughened tone. 'I like him well enough, but it knotted me up inside whenever I saw you with him.'

'Me and Nathan?' Did he actually care about her enough to be jealous? A warm glow started inside her. 'You really thought that we were a couple?'

'Something like that.' He scowled, his eyes darkening.

Katie laughed. 'He's just a very good friend and neighbour. He's been wonderful, giving me advice about the complaint and helping out with Jessica from time to time.'

'I wondered about that, too. I know how important Jessica is to you and she seemed to get on much better with Nathan than with me.' He frowned, running his hand along her spine and sending ripples of pleasure cascading through her body. 'Then you weren't here when I called and I guessed that you must have gone back home. Is that what you're planning to do? I know how much you care about Jessica, but I was hoping that you would stay on here.'

She looked up at him. 'She thought I wouldn't want her around if you were with me.'

He nodded. 'I thought she was feeling a bit awkward whenever we were together. You know, Katie, I love you, and if that means that your family comes along with you, that's fine by me. Jessica is your flesh and blood, and I would be more than happy to have her in my life.'

'You love me?' A smile broke out on her mouth. 'Do you really love me?'

'I really, really love you,' he said with a chuckle. 'Let me kiss you and show you just how much I love you.'

His mouth swooped down to capture hers, and for a long, long while she savoured that kiss. It made her toes curl in blissful excitement and sent quivers of exquisite delight to tease every nerve ending in her body. She ran her hands over his chest, along his shoulders and arms, loving the feel of him.

'That is a whole lot of love,' she said on a ragged sigh.

'Buckets full.' He looked down into her eyes, his mouth curving with amusement. 'Will you marry me, Katie? Please, say that you will.'

'I will.' She kissed him tenderly on the mouth. 'I definitely will.'

He rained kisses down on her, covering her cheeks, her forehead, her throat and then her mouth, before he eased back a little and contented himself with trailing a finger over the line of her jaw.

'What will you do about being with your family?' he asked. 'Do you want us to move back to Humberside? I'd prefer to stay here, now that I've been offered the post of head of the unit, but if you really want to be close to them, I'll understand. It would mean coming back on a regular basis to see my mother and my aunt.'

'You got the job?' Her eyes grew large. 'Oh, Alex, I'm so pleased for you…and after all that trouble. Haven't you told management that you won't suspend me, or do they think it's all working out for the best?'

'I told them I wasn't going to suspend you because I didn't see that you had done anything wrong, and I would prove it to them. I said we had to alter the way we view hospital practice with regard to inexperienced staff, and if I was going to be in charge things would be run the way I wanted them to be run.' He laughed. 'To be honest, I think they were too flummoxed to say very much at the time…but later they said the vote was unanimous. I was offered the job. I have to give them my answer tomorrow.'

She smiled up at him. 'Tell them you'll take it.' She

nestled her cheek against the crook of his shoulder. 'Actually, my parents are planning on moving here. They want to try their hand at property developing, and they have their eye on a sweet little property not too far from here as their first project. I've been to have a look at it, and it should work out quite well for them.'

'That's brilliant news. Of course, their next project could always be this cottage, couldn't it? I mean, it won't be big enough for us, will it? And if you don't like my place, then we'll have a look around and see what we can find. So that would possibly make project number three. Do you think they'll go for it?'

'Like a shot.' She lifted a hand to his face. 'Tell me again how much you love me.'

'I will…with pleasure.' He wrapped her in his arms and brushed his lips over hers. 'I love you this much… and this much…and…' And after that they didn't speak at all for a very long time.

0108 Gen Std HB

# FEBRUARY 2008 HARDBACK TITLES

## ROMANCE

|  |  |
|---|---|
| **The Italian Billionaire's Pregnant Bride** *Lynne Graham* | 978 0 263 20238 0 |
| **The Guardian's Forbidden Mistress** *Miranda Lee* | 978 0 263 20239 7 |
| **Secret Baby, Convenient Wife** *Kim Lawrence* | 978 0 263 20240 3 |
| **Caretti's Forced Bride** *Jennie Lucas* | 978 0 263 20241 0 |
| **The Salvatore Marriage Deal** *Natalie Rivers* | 978 0 263 20242 7 |
| **The British Billionaire Affair** *Susanne James* | 978 0 263 20243 4 |
| **One-Night Love-Child** *Anne McAllister* | 978 0 263 20244 1 |
| **Virgin: Wedded at the Italian's Convenience** *Diana Hamilton* | 978 0 263 20245 8 |
| **The Bride's Baby** *Liz Fielding* | 978 0 263 20246 5 |
| **Expecting a Miracle** *Jackie Braun* | 978 0 263 20247 2 |
| **Wedding Bells at Wandering Creek** *Patricia Thayer* | 978 0 263 20248 9 |
| **The Loner's Guarded Heart** *Michelle Douglas* | 978 0 263 20249 6 |
| **Sweetheart Lost and Found** *Shirley Jump* | 978 0 263 20250 2 |
| **The Single Dad's Patchwork Family** *Claire Baxter* | 978 0 263 20251 9 |
| **His Island Bride** *Marion Lennox* | 978 0 263 20252 6 |
| **Desert Prince, Expectant Mother** *Olivia Gates* | 978 0 263 20253 3 |

## HISTORICAL

|  |  |
|---|---|
| **Lady Gwendolen Investigates** *Anne Ashley* | 978 0 263 20189 5 |
| **The Unknown Heir** *Anne Herries* | 978 0 263 20190 1 |
| **Forbidden Lord** *Helen Dickson* | 978 0 263 20191 8 |

## MEDICAL™

|  |  |
|---|---|
| **The Doctor's Royal Love-Child** *Kate Hardy* | 978 0 263 19867 6 |
| **A Consultant Beyond Compare** *Joanna Neil* | 978 0 263 19871 3 |
| **The Surgeon Boss's Bride** *Melanie Milburne* | 978 0 263 19875 1 |
| **A Wife Worth Waiting For** *Maggie Kingsley* | 978 0 263 19879 9 |

0108 Gen Std LP

Pure reading pleasure

# FEBRUARY 2008 LARGE PRINT TITLES

## ROMANCE

| | |
|---|---|
| **The Greek Tycoon's Virgin Wife** *Helen Bianchin* | 978 0 263 20018 8 |
| **Italian Boss, Housekeeper Bride** *Sharon Kendrick* | 978 0 263 20019 5 |
| **Virgin Bought and Paid For** *Robyn Donald* | 978 0 263 20020 1 |
| **The Italian Billionaire's Secret Love-Child** *Cathy Williams* | 978 0 263 20021 8 |
| **The Mediterranean Rebel's Bride** *Lucy Gordon* | 978 0 263 20022 5 |
| **Found: Her Long-Lost Husband** *Jackie Braun* | 978 0 263 20023 2 |
| **The Duke's Baby** *Rebecca Winters* | 978 0 263 20024 9 |
| **Millionaire to the Rescue** *Ally Blake* | 978 0 263 20025 6 |

## HISTORICAL

| | |
|---|---|
| **Masquerading Mistress** *Sophia James* | 978 0 263 20121 5 |
| **Married By Christmas** *Anne Herries* | 978 0 263 20125 3 |
| **Taken By the Viking** *Michelle Styles* | 978 0 263 20129 1 |

## MEDICAL™

| | |
|---|---|
| **The Italian GP's Bride** *Kate Hardy* | 978 0 263 19932 1 |
| **The Consultant's Italian Knight** *Maggie Kingsley* | 978 0 263 19933 8 |
| **Her Man of Honour** *Melanie Milburne* | 978 0 263 19934 5 |
| **One Special Night...** *Margaret McDonagh* | 978 0 263 19935 2 |
| **The Doctor's Pregnancy Secret** *Leah Martyn* | 978 0 263 19936 9 |
| **Bride for a Single Dad** *Laura Iding* | 978 0 263 19937 6 |

# MARCH 2008 HARDBACK TITLES

## ROMANCE

|  |  |
|---|---|
| **The Markonos Bride** *Michelle Reid* | 978 0 263 20254 0 |
| **The Italian's Passionate Revenge** *Lucy Gordon* | 978 0 263 20255 7 |
| **The Greek Tycoon's Baby Bargain** *Sharon Kendrick* | 978 0 263 20256 4 |
| **Di Cesare's Pregnant Mistress** *Chantelle Shaw* | 978 0 263 20257 1 |
| **The Billionaire's Virgin Mistress** *Sandra Field* | 978 0 263 20258 8 |
| **At the Sicilian Count's Command** *Carole Mortimer* | 978 0 263 20259 5 |
| **Blackmailed For Her Baby** *Elizabeth Power* | 978 0 263 20260 1 |
| **The Cattle Baron's Virgin Wife** *Lindsay Armstrong* | 978 0 263 20261 8 |
| **His Pregnant Housekeeper** *Caroline Anderson* | 978 0 263 20262 5 |
| **The Italian Playboy's Secret Son** *Rebecca Winters* | 978 0 263 20263 2 |
| **Her Sheikh Boss** *Carol Grace* | 978 0 263 20264 9 |
| **Wanted: White Wedding** *Natasha Oakley* | 978 0 263 20265 6 |
| **The Heir's Convenient Wife** *Myrna Mackenzie* | 978 0 263 20266 3 |
| **Coming Home to the Cattleman** *Judy Christenberry* | 978 0 263 20267 0 |
| **Billionaire Doctor, Ordinary Nurse** *Carol Marinelli* | 978 0 263 20268 7 |
| **The Sheikh Surgeon's Baby** *Meredith Webber* | 978 0 263 20269 4 |

## HISTORICAL

|  |  |
|---|---|
| **The Last Rake In London** *Nicola Cornick* | 978 0 263 20192 5 |
| **The Outrageous Lady Felsham** *Louise Allen* | 978 0 263 20193 2 |
| **An Unconventional Miss** *Dorothy Elbury* | 978 0 263 20194 9 |

## MEDICAL™

|  |  |
|---|---|
| **Nurse Bride, Bayside Wedding** *Gill Sanderson* | 978 0 263 19883 6 |
| **The Outback Doctor's Surprise Bride** *Amy Andrews* | 978 0 263 19887 4 |
| **A Wedding at Limestone Coast** *Lucy Clark* | 978 0 263 19888 1 |
| **The Doctor's Meant-To-Be Marriage** *Janice Lynn* | 978 0 263 19889 8 |

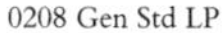


# MARCH 2008 LARGE PRINT TITLES

## ROMANCE

| | |
|---|---|
| **The Billionaire's Captive Bride** *Emma Darcy* | 978 0 263 20026 3 |
| **Bedded, or Wedded?** *Julia James* | 978 0 263 20027 0 |
| **The Boss's Christmas Baby** *Trish Morey* | 978 0 263 20028 7 |
| **The Greek Tycoon's Unwilling Wife** *Kate Walker* | 978 0 263 20029 4 |
| **Winter Roses** *Diana Palmer* | 978 0 263 20030 0 |
| **The Cowboy's Christmas Proposal** *Judy Christenberry* | 978 0 263 20031 7 |
| **Appointment at the Altar** *Jessica Hart* | 978 0 263 20032 4 |
| **Caring for His Baby** *Caroline Anderson* | 978 0 263 20033 1 |

## HISTORICAL

| | |
|---|---|
| **Scandalous Lord, Rebellious Miss** *Deb Marlowe* | 978 0 263 20133 8 |
| **The Duke's Gamble** *Miranda Jarrett* | 978 0 263 20137 6 |
| **The Damsel's Defiance** *Meriel Fuller* | 978 0 263 20141 3 |

## MEDICAL™

| | |
|---|---|
| **The Single Dad's Marriage Wish** *Carol Marinelli* | 978 0 263 19938 3 |
| **The Playboy Doctor's Proposal** *Alison Roberts* | 978 0 263 19939 0 |
| **The Consultant's Surprise Child** *Joanna Neil* | 978 0 263 19940 6 |
| **Dr Ferrero's Baby Secret** *Jennifer Taylor* | 978 0 263 19941 3 |
| **Their Very Special Child** *Dianne Drake* | 978 0 263 19942 0 |
| **The Surgeon's Runaway Bride** *Olivia Gates* | 978 0 263 19943 7 |